FRESHMAN

IN '59

D0860750

FRESHMAN IN '59

FRANCINE BUONO MOODY

TATE PUBLISHING
AND ENTERPRISES, LLC

Published by Tate Publishing & Enterprises, LLC
127 E. Trade Center Terrace | Mustang, Oklahoma 73064 USA
1.888.361.9473 | www.tatepublishing.com

Tate Publishing is committed to excellence in the publishing industry. The company reflects the philosophy established by the founders, based on Psalm 68:11,
"The Lord gave the word and great was the company of those who published it."

Book design copyright © 2013 by Tate Publishing, LLC. All rights reserved.
Cover design by Junriel Boquecosa
Interior design by Jomel Pepito

Published in the United States of America

ISBN: 978-1-62854-144-1
1. Fiction / Coming Of Age
2. Fiction / General
13.10.03

DEDICATION

 o my mother, my first teacher, and constant inspiration, Harriet Schuster Buono

ACKNOWLEDGMENTS

I wish to acknowledge family members, past and present, without whom this book could not have been written. My parents, Frank and Harriet Buono, first of all, who have always encouraged me in all my scholastic endeavors. My brother, Frank Buono, Jr., who still loves me in spite of "sibling differences." My husband, Howard Moody, who has supported me in many ways throughout this writing endeavor. My son, Neil Joseph Moody, who has provided technical support. My grandchildren, Matthew Stephan Sheaffer and Alicia Janae Sheaffer, who assisted me with computer knowledge (Matthew) and review of the initial manuscript as it was being written (Alicia).

I greatly appreciate the work of Stan Schoonmaker, retired history teacher and member of Dover Area Historical Society.

Also, the encouragement and questions answered by my long-time high school friend Ann Haddock Downing have been invaluable.

Reverend Elbridge T. Holland's contributions to the accuracy of spiritual elements are gratefully acknowledged. As retired Methodist pastor and district superintendent his knowledge is much valued.

And to my editor, Rachael Sweeden, Laura Hawkins, and all the people at Tate Publishing, with whom I have had the privilege of working, I say a big Thank You!

AUTHOR'S NOTE

This book is based on actual entries from my diary, written about my freshman year in Dover High School, Dover, New Jersey, from June of 1959 through May of 1960. It seemed appropriate to tell this story in 2013 since my fellow students and I, who began this journey in 1959 and graduated in 1963, will celebrate our fiftieth anniversary this year.

While grounded in fact and written with every attempt to be historically accurate, much of the story is fiction. Names of places and events have been used as they were then used, but characters and their names are fictitious.

It is hoped that the story will provide a window into the past for the freshmen of today and lovely recollections of wonderful memories for the freshmen of 1959.

THE DIARY

On a bright, sunny Saturday afternoon in June, Anne Duncan, her dark chestnut flip blowing out behind her slender shoulders, hurried down Prospect Street toward downtown Dover. She didn't want to be late to meet her best friend, Jenny Smith. Anne was to meet Jenny at the back entrance to the big, new J.J. Newberry store. Crossing the railroad tracks, she had only two short blocks to go when she spotted Jen's bright copper auburn pageboy, making her instantly recognizable from the rest of the crowd milling around the doors to the department store.

The five dollars her grandmother had given Anne as a graduation present was "burning a hole in her pocket," her mother had said. She already knew what she wanted to buy; she had been thinking for a while that a diary might be exciting to have now that she'd be entering high school in September. The idea had solidified in her mind after getting the gift of money from her grandmother the previous night. It was a lot of money for her grandmother to give, Anne knew, and a lot for her to spend. It would have taken her a long time to save that much with her twenty-five-cent weekly allowance. In the small suburban town of Dover in 1959, there was no way for her at thirteen years old to earn the money. Her parents had said she might start babysitting at fourteen, but that was six months away yet. At sixteen, she might be able to work at Newberry's for a dollar an hour, but right now, money was not easy to obtain. So, she was very grateful for her grandmother's generosity.

Reaching the beginning of the last block now, Anne called out to Jenny.

Jenny turned her head toward Anne's voice and waved.

Approaching Jenny, Anne said, "Hi, Jen. Have you been here long?"

"Hi, Anne. No, I just got here a few minutes ago. Are you ready to make your big purchase?"

"Yes, I've been looking forward to buying a diary for a while," Anne said as she nodded her head in agreement and pulled open the heavy glass door she had now reached.

Jenny followed Anne into the store and they went quickly to the stationery counter, passing the long, gleaming white lunch counter, a usual Saturday stop, without even a glance. Jenny and Anne searched the shelves with intense eyes.

Jenny held up a tiny, white, leather-covered volume with gold edges. "How about this?" she asked.

Anne politely answered, "It's certainly pretty, but too small, I think."

Anne next discarded a brown, leather-book, but then, she saw a maroon-covered volume with gold lettering on the front describing it as a "five-year diary." That was intriguing. With that, she could record events from all of her high school experience and even into her freshman year in college, which she hoped to attend. As she picked up the diary to examine it, she noticed it had a brass lock holding it closed and a tiny brass key attached to it. That clinched it for Anne. To be able to write whatever she wanted and to keep those thoughts private by locking the book was a marvelous idea.

"This is perfect," she told Jenny, who was looking at stationery on the next shelf.

"Great," Jenny replied. Holding up a packet of flowered writing paper with matching envelopes, she added, "I think I'll get this."

Behind Jenny, next to the stationery, Anne noticed some fancy pens. Since the diary was $2.95, she could also buy a pen. She chose a long, white, plastic ballpoint pen.

As they carried their finds to the closest cashier, they again passed the lunch counter. This time, Jenny looked over and noticed a sign advertising Cherry Cokes as a special for that day at twenty-five cents.

"Anne," Jenny called out as Anne continued walking toward the cashier. "Let's stop for a Coke, my treat."

"O…okay," Anne slowly replied. "As soon as we pay for our things." She was eager to get home and start writing, but she didn't want to rush her friend.

The two girls found the cashier, paid for their purchases, and carried their brown paper bags back to the lunch counter. After climbing up onto the high round stools, Jenny gave their orders to the waitress. A few minutes later, as they sipped their sodas, Anne twirled around on the revolving stool to survey a large group of customers thronged around a sales table. What was so special? Was there anyone she knew?

There was one tall, familiar figure, standing out among the others, at least a head taller than everyone else. It had to be John Jones. Anne had been friends with John since fourth grade. They had been in Mr. Cline's class together at Academy Street School. And at the sixth grade graduation dance he had danced every dance with her. But they really were only good friends. Anne had no romantic notions about John or any other boy. Her parents discouraged that and she felt she had plenty of time for that later. The dance had been fun, though, and John was a lot of fun. He didn't act as if he were interested in dating now either. So, they could just have fun together.

All those thoughts had come very quickly to Anne and just as she was turning to tell Jenny she had seen John, he saw her and waved. Loping over with his long stride, John was next to them in a minute. "Hi, Ann-ee!" John exclaimed, with a big grin spreading from ear to ear. He knew Anne didn't like the nickname, but he always said it with such good-natured affection that she accepted it, only from him, in the same manner.

"Hi, John," Anne replied brightly. "You know Jenny from school last year," Anne added politely, including her friend in the conversation.

"Sure," John answered, smiling at Jenny too.

Jenny nodded in acknowledgement. "Hi, John."

"So, what are you girls up to?" John questioned, looking directly at Anne.

"We were just out spending some of our graduation money," Anne told him, not willing to let him, or anyone else except Jenny, know she had bought a diary. "And what are you doing, John?" Anne quickly asked in order to keep him from questioning further.

A little red in the face, John—nevertheless—answered, "My mother wanted me to come down and look at the men's socks on sale. My size thirteen feet are expensive for shoes, and socks, too."

Anne decided not to ask if he had found what he wanted. As he didn't carry a brown paper bag, she did not want to embarrass him, and she did not want him to ask what she had purchased. "Well, I really have to be going home. I promised my mother that I'd make this a fast trip so I could get home and help with supper."

"Me too," John told her. "I'll walk you part of the way."

Anne quickly looked at Jenny to see how she felt about that. Jenny knew John was just a long-time, childhood friend. She'd only known Anne two years since they had just met in seventh grade at the new junior high where they all had to go now. Jenny knew, too, that John and Anne both lived in the same direction since they had attended the same elementary school. She easily answered Anne's look with, "That's fine. I have to go, too. We can't walk together anyhow since we live in two different directions. I'll call you tonight."

The girls climbed down from the high stools and started for the door with John following behind. At the door, Jenny repeated, "I'll call you tonight," and turned right.

Anne and John turned to the left and walked down the street toward their homes.

"So, not long now until we're out of prison and in the big, bad high school, huh, Anne? How do you feel about it?" John questioned Anne.

"John!" Anne exclaimed in mock protest. "I don't think you really should call our junior high a prison! It was rather rigid the way we all had to go in long lines from class to class. And, I do think we will feel more independent in high school, but on the other hand, we might have a hard time finding our classes."

"Yeah, we might, but I'm really looking forward to it. It's going to be fun. I'm planning on trying out for the football team, too."

"That's great, John," Anne encouraged. "All the Academy Street School kids will be so proud of you and cheer for you. But I'm still worried about not finding my classes. I think I might go over to the high school in the summer once I get my schedule and try to find my classes, just kind of practice ahead of time."

Now it was John's turn to encourage Anne. "That's a good idea, Anne. In fact, I might do that, too. If I don't suggest it, my mother probably will."

"Your mother is a very caring person, John. If she says to do something, it's just to help you." Anne reprimanded him.

"I know," John sheepishly admitted. "Well, here's where we go our separate ways. Hope you have a great summer, Anne."

"Thanks, John, you too," Anne called out after him as he turned to the right and she turned to the left toward home. As she walked alone, she thought of what she would write as her first entry in her diary. It would be about the diary, of course, and Jenny; maybe John's confidence; and her fear about going to high school.

That night, Anne pulled out the new diary and pen from the drawer in her desk and began writing.

Dear Diary,

Today, Jenny and I went shopping. I got this diary and the pen I write with at Newberry's, with money my grandmother gave me for graduation. I saw John and he's not worried about finding high school classes, but I am. I wonder what high school will be like.

Love,
Anne

OLD FRIENDS

Make new friends but keep the old. One is silver, the other is gold." Anne hummed the tune as she dusted the furniture in her bedroom. She remembered having sung it at Girl Scout meetings for several years. She reflected on the words. It seemed to be conveying the message that a girl should try to make new friends, but also keep the old ones because the new ones were valuable, like silver. But the old friends should be kept because they were even more valuable, like gold. Well, she was certainly hanging on to the old ones. Having a pajama party tonight for her old girlfriends was doing just that. She hadn't even made any new friends recently. Maybe she would when she got to the high school. There was that girl she had met at graduation. After their chorus had finished singing "Let There Be Peace on Earth," they had walked off the stage, and there she was, wearing the same pink, dotted organdy dress as Anne. They had just stared at each other and smiled. Maybe she would get to know her in high school.

"Anne," her mother called up the stairs. "How are you doing up there?"

"Almost finished, Mom," Anne yelled back.

"Well, as soon as you do finish, come down and help me with things down here."

"Okay."

Anne hurried to finish dusting the big, old oak dresser. She'd already done the big double bed and desk. She remade the bed with the clean flowered sheets, pulled the mint green bedspread over it, and looked around in satisfaction. It certainly wasn't fancy, but it was clean and neat.

With three sleeping bags on the floor, there'd be space for five of them to sleep. Jenny, of course, was coming. Sandy Bettins and Sally Vale, from church, and Jane Gordon, her long-time friend from Academy Street, completed the list. She was so glad Jane was able to come since her family had moved away to live with her grandmother. She didn't have the opportunity to see Jane very often. She hoped they all would like each other.

Jane was to come at five for supper. The other girls were to arrive at seven. They'd do their nails, set their hair, get into pajamas, and watch TV. She was so glad that two of her favorite programs were on tonight: *Father Knows Best* and *Leave it to Beaver*. Bud and Wally were really dreamy and she learned so much from popular Betty. They had real-life problems, and they worked them out in good ways.

"Anne!" her mother called out loudly. "I need you."

"Coming!" Anne yelled back, as she quickly left her reverie and hurried down the hall and down the stairs to the kitchen.

"It's already 4:30, Anne," her mother said as Anne came into the kitchen. "Please get the french fries and fish out of the freezer and put them in the oven, while I put the carrots on to cook. Then set the dining room table. Since Jane is coming for supper, we'll eat in there instead of in the kitchen. As soon as we eat supper, we'll have to do the dishes and get the kitchen cleaned up. I'll get the popcorn out for you to pop later."

Anne dashed to the freezer and was able to pull open the top door to get the french fries and fish out while her mother opened the door to the refrigerator below to get out the carrots.

Anne first turned on the oven, then poured out the fries and fish from their cardboard boxes onto the baking sheets, and pushed them into the oven. Grabbing silverware from the drawer next to the sink, she ran to the dining room and plopped utensils down into four places.

She was glad her brother would be spending the night with his friend Marv. The girls would not be bothered with his antics. Her mother simply explained that she did not want a bunch of teenage girls and boys in the house at the same time. Just as she finished putting out the last fork, the doorbell rang.

Anne ran to the front hall and opened the door wide. There stood Jane, just as she remembered her: long, light brown, wavy hair; petite and pretty. Even though they had not seen each other in more than a year since the Gordon family had moved away, they fell into each other's arms, hugging and laughing.

"Jane!" Anne managed to exclaim. "You look wonderful! She stepped back and added, "Come on in."

As Jane and Mrs. Gordon walked inside, Anne's mother came in from the kitchen, wiping her hands on her apron. "It's so good to see you both. How was your trip?"

"Just fine, not too much traffic at this time. But I will hurry right back if you don't mind so that I don't get into the work traffic going home. It took about an hour so I want to get back for supper with Jim," Janice Gordon responded.

"Oh, I understand, although I wish you didn't have to hurry and could stay and visit," Mrs. Duncan replied.

"We can visit when you bring Jane back tomorrow afternoon. Will you be able to then? Are you sure you still want to make that trip? We can come and get her."

"We are planning on it. You brought her and we'll take her back. We can get there in the middle of the afternoon, being Saturday, and we can visit an hour or so before we have to head back."

"Great, we'll see you then." Mrs. Gordon turned to leave. Giving Jane a hug as she went out the door, she added, "Have a great time!"

Anne closed the door and, picking up Jane's small suitcase from where Mrs. Gordon had put it down, she headed up the stairs. "Come on, Jane, we'll just put your things up in my room."

Jane followed Anne up the stairs, as Mrs. Duncan hurried back to the kitchen, calling out after them, "Don't be long. Supper will be ready in about ten minutes."

A short while later, all gathered at the table, Mr. Duncan led them in thanking God for the meal and expressing thanks, too, for Jane and the other girls being able to be there with them.

As they ate, Anne filled Jane in on the plans. "Right after supper, we can make popcorn. Then, I thought as soon as the others get here we'll get into pajamas and do our nails. While they dry we can watch TV, and then we can play records and dance. What do you think, Jane?"

"Sounds great to me. I brought all my Ricky Nelson records."

"Wonderful! You know he's my favorite."

Being too excited to eat much, the girls hurried through supper, cleared the dishes, and put them in the sink to wash.

"Don't bother with the dishes, Anne," Mrs. Duncan directed as she started filling the sink with water. "I'll do them while you make the popcorn."

"Thanks, Mom," Anne gratefully replied as she pulled a large pot out of the cabinet. Setting it on the stove, she poured in some oil, and turned the heat to medium.

As soon as the oil was hot, Anne poured in enough popcorn kernels to cover the bottom of the pan, covered it, and put butter into a large metal bowl. When she heard the popping starting, she shook the pan vigorously. As soon as the popping stopped, she poured the popcorn onto the butter and placed the metal bowl on the turned off electric burner, stirred it a few times, and covered it with foil to keep warm.

She heard the doorbell ringing as she was covering the bowl. Now, she heard the voices of Jenny, Sandy, and Sally as her father opened the door.

Going into the hall with Jane, she exclaimed, "Well, that was perfect. You all arrived together and exactly on time! Let me introduce you to my old elementary school friend, Jane."

Pointing to her auburn-haired friend, Anne said, "Jane, this is Jenny. Sandy, the blonde, is behind her, and Sally is the brunette at the end."

"Hi," the usually effervescent Jane said, rather shyly.

"Everyone, take your things up to my room," Anne instructed. "We've got the popcorn ready, so I think we'll just get into pajamas and come back down to do our nails while we watch TV. Then, we'll play some records and dance."

"Yay! " All the girls shouted and dashed upstairs.

Three hours later, as they all crowded into Anne's room to try to quiet down and get a little sleep, Anne asked, "How do you all feel about starting high school in a few weeks?"

"I'll be glad to see my friends again," Jane responded.

Also going to a different school than the other three, Sandy said, "I haven't seen most of my classmates this summer either. Living out in the country, I usually only get to see Sally and Anne and the other girls who will go to Dover High School here, on Sundays in Sunday School class, or choir. But my school is really big so I am a little scared."

Jenny and Sally were quiet.

Anne continued the conversation. "Well, Jenny and I saw John at the beginning of the summer and he was really eager, but I am rather anxious. Do you think boys might be braver than we are?"

"Well, I think they might not want to admit that they are a little scared, but maybe they really feel just the way we do," Jane said.

"Yeah," they all agreed. Even Jenny and Sally piped up with their agreement to this belief.

"Well, I do hope we all can stay friends. But, it will be nice to make new friends, too, won't it?" Anne questioned her friends.

"Yes," three voices again agreed. Jenny was already asleep.

"I guess we all better get some sleep," Anne told them. As she drifted off, she thought about what she would write in her diary the next day. It had been a great day, seeing Jane, having a party, and everyone seeming to feel the same way about high school coming in a few weeks. They all were a little anxious.

FIRST DAYS
OF HIGH SCHOOL

September 10, the first day of high school, seemed to come all too soon for the anxious Anne. Even though Labor Day was late this year and school always started after Labor Day, the first day of high school had arrived all too fast. At least, she had come last week with her schedule in hand, to find her classrooms. So, this morning, she was able to find her homeroom quite easily. Even her locker combination had not been hard to work since she had practiced it a number of times. But now, sitting here in homeroom, there were a lot of unfamiliar faces.

Anne knew that homerooms were composed of about thirty students each, listed alphabetically. With her last name beginning with *D*, near the beginning of the alphabet, John and Jenny were not in this homeroom with her. Sally was also in another room. They weren't even in any classes with her. They all had compared their schedules as soon as they had arrived in the mail. She wasn't surprised that Jenny and Sally were not in classes with her since she was in the college preparatory program and they had chosen the business education program. But John had also chosen the college preparatory program since he also wanted to be a teacher as she did. And they still were not in any classes together!

Anne fervently prayed a silent prayer that someone she knew from junior high would be in each of her classes, especially gym class. There would be so many girls in that class and, to her mind, probably all very athletic. Reading was her "thing," not sports. She always felt like a klutz. It would be so good to have a friend there.

All too soon, all the announcements were made and all the forms "to be completed by parents and returned tomorrow" stowed away. The bell rang and they were on their way to their first classes.

The whole day had passed in a whirl, Anne reflected at her locker at the end of the day. Looking over her assignment pad, she chose the books she needed to take home to do the homework required for Tuesday. She felt so alone. John had taken a yellow school bus home, living more than the required two miles from the school. Sally lived more than two miles in the opposite direction, so she had also hurried to a bus. Anne lived just a little less than two miles so she needed to start her long walk soon.

"Hey, Anne! How was it today?" Jenny burst out, as she came rushing up to Anne.

"Jenny! I forgot you would be walking home, too. I wish we lived in the same direction. Well, I guess the day was all right. Everything went so fast and there's so much to remember. How did it go for you?"

"Good! Sally is in typing with me. I know what you mean about going so fast. There's a lot to learn: schedules, locations, rules. One thing that does look like fun, though, are these beanies. The orange does clash with my hair, but I knew orange and black are the school colors, so I'll just have to live with it."

"I don't mind the colors, but I don't like the idea of upperclassmen being able to know who the freshmen are and maybe giving us a hard time."

"Well, there are neat things with them, too, like Tiger Day and the dance on the twenty-sixth. Do you want to go together?" Jenny asked.

"Sure, we can plan on going together and hope some boys ask us to dance," Anne answered. "Well, I'm glad I got to see you, but I'd better hurry now so I can get started on all this homework. I think I have something in every subject."

"That's the good thing about my classes. They don't expect you to be able to practice typing at home. I do have some business math and an English assignment too, though. I have to go too. See you tomorrow." Jenny waved goodbye.

"I'll call you later," Anne called out as she started walking down the hall, toward the front door. "We can talk about what we might wear to the dance."

"Great!" Jenny yelled back as she walked out the back door.

As she trudged up the long hill toward home, Anne worried about all the homework she had to get done before tomorrow. "Cast all your anxieties on him, for he cares for you," She quoted aloud. "I think that's 1 Peter 5:7," she continued. She asked God to help her to not worry. She determined to start on the homework as soon as she arrived home, taking one thing at a time and just working her way through it. Then she turned her thoughts to good memories of the day.

One good memory certainly was a handsome boy she had met in world history class. He'd sat right across the aisle from her and had smiled brightly at her when he sat down. He was tall, thin, and had wavy brown hair. He seemed quite studious as he paid close attention to Mr. Collins and wrote down notes in a big, blue notebook. She'd learned his name since he had followed her to English class next. Jeff Erickson. It seemed to fit him. So, they were in two classes together. Now, she thought she remembered seeing him in homeroom also. Anne hoped they would get to be friends.

Late that evening, she was very tired, as her homework had taken a long time to do. She glanced at the clock with sleepy eyes. Ten o'clock! She had only taken time to eat supper and hadn't even called Jenny as she had promised. Even hurrying, she would not be ready for bed until ten thirty. Tomorrow morning would come quickly.

Thirty minutes later, she almost fell into bed, only taking time to pray a quick prayer for her family, not even thinking of writing in her diary.

Anne soon fell into a routine of classes and homework, feeling as if she only had time to relax on weekends. She felt she didn't even have time as yet to make any new friends, although Jeff did smile at her each day in classes. And, there was a girl in her gym class who seemed very nice, but maybe shy. Anne thought her name was Alice and she hoped they might become friends.

Thankfully, Anne still had Jenny as a friend, but the only time she saw her during the day was lunchtime and that was only about twenty minutes. They usually did get together on weekends, and they were going to Saturday afternoon football games, but that was about all they could manage now.

Two weeks had flown by so quickly! Anne was looking forward to some fun today. Today was Tiger Day, named for the school mascot. They were to be dismissed from school early to walk over to the football field. She couldn't even manage to walk with Jenny. They would be walking over with their homeroom classes and sitting with them. At least Jeff would be there. Maybe he'd talk to her finally!

Anne didn't know exactly what to expect, but she knew the football players would be introduced and the freshman queen would be chosen. They all had been able to vote for a queen. She was very proud that she personally knew a football player and a queen nominee from her elementary school. John was on the freshman football squad and beautiful Pat Strickler was a nominee for queen. Pat was such a lovely girl, beautiful on the inside as well as the outside, and always friendly to everyone. With her gorgeous, long black hair and gleaming smile, everyone would think she looked like a queen, Anne thought. But more than that, Anne knew Pat was kind and warm. Pat lived on the other side of Academy Street School and in fifth grade had ridden her bicycle the four blocks over to Anne's house so they could ride bikes together. Anne really hoped Pat would get chosen to be queen. She deserved the honor.

Now, they all were being instructed by the teachers to crowd together, staying with their classes on the cold metal bleachers. The school band played marches and their school song. The high school principal, Mr. Spurgeon, welcomed everyone and told the freshmen what high expectations the faculty had for them. It sounded good and Anne felt proud to be part of this freshman class, but she wanted to hear who was chosen queen!

Next, the football players were introduced as each one ran onto the field. John was the tallest one there, Anne noted with satisfaction. There were some who came close, however.

Finally, Mr. Spurgeon announced that the freshman queen would be named. He said it had been a close race and all the girls were lovely, but one had come out on top. And that one was Pat Strickler! Anne cheered loudly as did everyone around her, even if they weren't from her elementary school. Anne was sure they all had seen Pat's kindness as well as her beauty. She was very happy for Pat. Mr. Spurgeon dismissed the students to walk back to the school to catch busses and to walk home.

Anne walked home happy for Pat, but a little sad for herself. Jeff had not talked to her at all!

She went to sleep that night thinking about the dance the next day, after school. She hoped that at least Jeff would ask her to dance.

The next morning, Anne dressed carefully for school since she'd be staying after school for the dance. When her mother had heard about the dance, she'd expected Anne to wear one of the two new dresses she'd made for her. Anne appreciated her mother's work, but the bright flower print dresses really stood out from the skirts and blouses most of the other girls wore. Anne hated being conspicuous, but she didn't want to disappoint her mother, so she chose the lavender print. She'd try to hide behind Jenny.

Classes seemed to go slowly all day, but she dreamed of the dance, and her reverie helped the time to pass more quickly. Of course, she might have missed something, especially when Mrs. Penny lectured about *Ivanhoe*. Anne hoped she'd gotten all her assignments written down correctly. She'd have to review the classwork tonight. At last, it was time for the dance and as planned, Jenny met her at her locker. Anne admired Jenny's quiet-looking beige skirt and blouse. "You look great! I love that outfit. You go first into the gym."

"Thanks, my mother just bought it for me when we were in New York last week. Why do you want me to go first?" Jenny asked.

"I'm embarrassed by this bright print. I kind of want to hide. I do appreciate my mother's work, but you know me, I don't like to be conspicuous."

"You'll be fine," Jenny assured her. "If you hide, no boy will ask you to dance."

"I'll take my chances," Anne decided.

Later, riding home in the car with her mother, Anne was not so sure she had made the right decision.

"Why so downcast?" Mrs. Duncan asked.

"The dance was terrible. I didn't get asked to dance by any boys. Jenny is the only one I danced with. Most of the girls danced together, but a few danced with boys."

"Well, I see girls dancing together a lot on *American Bandstand*," Mrs. Duncan assured her daughter. "There will be other dances and you have plenty of time for boys later. You're still young."

Anne just sighed.

The following week, however, there was another dance and this time things were entirely different. As Anne reflected on it later, she decided she'd had a wonderful time. Jeff had asked her to dance two times! He'd even gotten some refreshments for her!

The next day at school, she felt was wonderful too! Jeff had carried her books for her from world history to English! Things were really looking up.

That night, she finally took time to write in her diary.

Dear Diary,

High school is pretty good. There is a lot of work, but there's a lot of fun, too. There are dances and football games. There was a terrible dance where no boy asked me to dance, but then this week there was a great dance where Jeff Erickson asked me to dance two times and the next day he carried my books. I think I'm going to really like high school.

Love,
Anne

"SILVER" AND "GOLD" FRIENDSHIPS

ow! That was a good game!" Anne exclaimed to Jenny as they climbed down from the bleachers to leave the football stadium.

"It sure was," Jenny replied. "It was really close until the fourth quarter. Your friend John came through with a great tackle and Rick made the final touchdown."

"Yeah, that's what you told me. That's right when I fell off the bleachers, I guess. At least it was only the second step. I'm glad we don't sit up high so we can easily walk up and down the track and see who is here. It certainly helped me out this time."

"So, that's why you sit there," came a voice from behind Anne.

Anne spun around to see who was talking, although she was sure she recognized the voice and already knew. There stood Jeff smiling broadly.

"Jeff, you spy, sneaking up on me like that," Anne chided him.

"I wasn't spying or sneaking, Anne," Jeff quickly defended himself in a teasing voice. "I only happened to be walking out behind you. I did speak up and did let you know I was here. Now, if I'd been spying on you, I would have kept quiet and probably could have found out a lot of juicy gossip."

"Oh, Jeff, you have such an analytical mind, to come up with that explanation," Anne mildly protested. "But you wouldn't have heard any juicy gossip. I don't spread gossip," Anne added.

"Well, now that's a revelation, and you certainly are an exception to your gender then," Jeff countered in an amazed tone.

"Thanks a lot!" Anne sarcastically answered and was about to say more when Jeff seemed alarmed as he saw something up ahead. "Hey! There's my ride! I have to hurry. See you on Monday!" Jeff yelled back at Anne as he ran toward the road up ahead of them. "Well, who was that, Anne? Or is he a secret?" Jenny asked.

Anne, suddenly brought back to earth, remembered Jenny was beside her. "Oh, Jenny, that was just Jeff. He's in two of my classes."

"Well, thanks for introducing me," Jenny replied in a voice brimming with sarcasm. "That's the same boy who was with you at the dance, isn't it? So that's the second time you didn't introduce me."

"Oh, Jenny, I'm sorry. Everything seems to happen so fast when Jeff's around. He suddenly shows up and then he's suddenly gone just as fast. I can't even think of anything else," Anne attempted to explain to her friend.

"Well, here's my house anyhow. I'll see you on Monday, I guess. Bye, Anne." And with that, Jenny quickly marched up the walk to her front door.

Anne was suddenly left to mull over all that had happened in the last, very fast ten minutes. Jenny lived so close to the football field. Normally, she would have invited her in for a while before she had to begin her long walk home. Mrs. Smith was always so kind, offering a snack, and maybe even a ride home. Jenny really must have been miffed. .Anne continued to try to figure out what had gone wrong as she slowly walked down the sidewalk. She seemed to have been on a roller coaster. She reviewed: she and Jenny had fun at the game. They were having a good time together. Then, Jeff showed up. The banter between them had been fun too. But suddenly he was gone and Jenny was angry with her. Anne reprimanded herself. She probably had been rude to Jenny, not introducing her to Jeff. But really, everything had happened so fast. Suddenly, Jeff was there and then suddenly he was gone. She really didn't have time to think of anything like introductions. She didn't even remember that Jenny was there until Jeff was gone!

Well, she'd certainly have to be more careful in the future. She didn't want to hurt Jenny's feelings. They had been friends for quite a while now. Anne did not want to lose her friendship.

Anne trudged homeward not only with a slightly heavy heart, but also with a resolve to make amends. Everything would be all right on Monday, she decided.

Monday came quickly. It always seemed as if the weekends did fly by so fast. Anne had determined to try to be extra attentive and kind to Jenny at lunchtime. But when she walked into the cafeteria, she didn't see Jenny at their usual meeting place. They always met just inside the doors, by the first table to the right. She scanned the large room, as far as she could see around the room nearly filled with noisy, rambunctious freshmen talking in groups and lining up at the kitchen doors.

Not finding Jenny, Anne went over to the milk line to purchase a carton of milk to go with her packed lunch. And, there was Alice, the last person in line, her dark brown ponytail recognizable, as Anne walked to the end of the line. Anne had been wanting to get to know her and now maybe she had an opportunity.

"Hi, Alice," Anne called out as she came up behind her. "How are you?"

Alice quickly turned to face Anne and, with a genuinely warm smile, replied, "I'm fine, Anne, how are you?"

"I'm fine, Alice. It's good to see you. I've never seen you at lunch before."

"Well, I usually get here earlier. We got dismissed from science later today."

"I guess I got here a little earlier than usual. I don't see my friend I usually eat with."

"Come and eat with us. We sit over on the far side of the room away from the hustle and bustle. This is my friend Janette," Alice said, as she tapped the girl in front of her on the shoulder.

"Janette, this is Anne, who's in my gym class," Alice introduced Anne as a pale, quiet-looking girl with light brown hair in a pageboy style turned around.

Lunch turned out to be a very pleasant respite in an otherwise dull day for Anne. She felt as if she'd made a new friend in Alice, maybe even two, as Janette seemed very friendly also. But she was still concerned about Jenny.

At the end of the day, Anne hurried to the other end of the hall to try to find Jenny. Hoping to catch her at her locker, she thought she'd invite her to go shopping on Saturday. When she got to the locker, though, Jenny was just walking toward the door to leave.

"Jen!" Anne called and hurried after her friend.

As she ran up to Jenny, she burst out, "I missed you at lunch today."

"Well, I got there later than usual and you were nowhere to be found."

"Oh Jenny, I'm sorry. I guess I got there earlier. I looked for you, but couldn't find you. I wanted to ask you if you would like to go shopping on Saturday."

"Oh, I'm going to be busy," Jenny answered quickly. "I have to hurry home," she added and turned back toward the door.

Anne, feeling bewildered, slowly turned in the opposite direction, toward the front door and on her way home. She reviewed the events of the day, as she walked. Jenny seemed to be angry with her. Or, at least she's awfully busy. Anne decided that she would ask Alice to go shopping with her.

The next day, at lunchtime, she didn't see Jenny again, so she looked for Alice. Finding her, Anne asked her if she would like to go shopping on Saturday. Alice quickly replied she would really like that.

After getting their milk, they walked to the back of the cafeteria where Janette was already waiting at a table. On their way, Anne asked if Alice thought Janette would want to go with them on Saturday. She didn't want to leave her out. Alice assured her that Janette undoubtedly would not be able to go. She had younger brothers and sisters and a lot of responsibilities at home.

As they came up to the table, Janette welcomed Anne with a big warm smile. Anne noticed that she looked pale and ate only a peanut butter and jelly sandwich, just as she had the day before. Anne decided she would bring an extra oatmeal raisin cookie tomorrow so that she'd have three and then be able to share with both girls.

On her way home at the end of the day, Anne reflected on how easy the friendship with Alice and Janette was, and hoped her friendship with Jenny didn't end. As she walked, she prayed a silent prayer, asking God to help her to be friends with all three girls. Immediately, the verse "A friend loves at all times," came to mind. She remembered it was Proverbs 17:17. She might look it up later, but right now it helps to see that I need to keep trying to hold on to the friendship with Jenny, she thought, and determined to call her later.

After supper and homework that evening, Anne decided to try one more time to revive the friendship with Jenny. She telephoned her and suggested that they meet for lunch at school the next day in their usual place and just wait for one another if they didn't arrive at the same time. Jenny seemed relieved that they were going to try to work things out and readily agreed to the solution.

The next day, Anne was pleased to see Jenny waiting in their usual spot when she arrived for lunch. They talked and laughed as they always had done in the past. When they went downstairs after lunch, the fun continued. Anne was still eating an apple and a hall monitor told them they had to return to the cafeteria. They went back up a few steps, out of sight, and Anne put the apple in her purse. Then, they proceeded back down and laughed so much that the hall monitor guessed the apple was still with Anne, but he had a laugh too and let them continue on their way outside until lunchtime was over.

Anne was very happy to see that Alice was still friendly too, when it was time for gym class. The class was going to the bowling alley today and Alice was her bowling partner. They had a lot of laughs over all their gutter balls and Anne didn't have to be embarrassed by her low score with Alice. Even though Alice did beat her, the scores were very close at 32 to 27!

As they went their separate ways, Alice reminded Anne that she'd meet her at Newberry's on Saturday at 1:00 p.m. Anne was happy to have Alice as a new friend, but she hoped she would not lose her friendship with Jenny.

When Anne woke up the next morning, she was almost thankful to see that it was raining. Walking downtown to shop was not something she or Alice would want to do in the rain. She called Alice and said she guessed they'd have to postpone the shopping trip. Alice readily agreed.

That night, Anne decided it was a good time to write in her diary, to reflect on her feelings about friends.

Dear Diary,

I really like Alice. She's a lot of fun and I'm really glad she's in my gym class. But I'm glad it rained today because I didn't want to take a chance on Jenny being angry with me again if I went shopping with Alice. I guess Alice is a "silver" friend and Jenny is a "gold" one. Both are valuable and I hope I can keep them both as friends.

Love,
Anne

A DIFFICULT TIME

The fall leaves crunched underneath Anne's feet as she walked down Morris Street toward the high school. Any other time she would have enjoyed the autumn colors all around her. The orange, yellow, and red leaves still hanging on the trees made a beautiful canopy above her. But today, she didn't even notice them. Today, her steps were heavy, and the crunch of the leaves under her feet seemed to reflect her mood.

Today was a gym day. And Anne was not happy about it. She carried a clean gym suit with her, but no amount of washing or ironing could change the way that ugly blue suit looked on her, she thought as she plodded along. All the girls seemed to think it was ugly. Maybe it looked all right on some girls, the "more mature-looking" ones, but on her, thin as she was, it just hung.

Not only did Anne feel ugly in that suit, but just thinking about gym class made her practically tremble. Bowling was not bad. Although she could not get a strike to save her life, she could bowl with Alice and have fun. She didn't have to be embarrassed in front of all the other girls. But today, they wouldn't bowl, as today began their basketball season. She didn't really mind basketball. In fact, she rather liked it. It was one sport she could understand. She liked watching other people play it. But she, Anne Duncan, had no athletic skill in any sport!

Now, Anne was almost to the school. She'd just have to be brave and get through it. Maybe if she tried to think of all the good things she possibly could, it would help. Number one, at least Alice would be there. She was also thin and not athletic. There would be at least two of them. Number two, gym class was before lunch, so she might have some good classes before it and she'd be able to talk to Alice after it if it was really bad. Just thinking that it might be really bad made her tremble again. So much for trying to think of good things. It wasn't working.

Just as Anne crossed the street to go down the sidewalk past the parking lot, a car approached the driveway and the driver waved at her! Lowering her head to peek in the window as the car went by, Anne saw that it was Mrs. Kane, waving and smiling at her. Anne waved back, and suddenly the day seemed brighter. Mrs. Kane was her science teacher and seemed to really like Anne. She had complimented

Anne on those bright print dresses. She was also the FTA advisor and encouraged Anne to join the club. At least she could look forward to fourth period and science class after third period gym class. That, and lunch, might help her to get over any distress gym class might create.

Anne climbed the steep concrete steps up to the main doors of the building and slipped into the front hall with a springier step. She hurried to her locker, stuffed her gym suit in, and rushed on down the hall as the first bell rang. Maybe gym class wouldn't be so bad. But now she'd have to hurry to get to homeroom on time. Joining the crowd of noisy, rushing students, Anne waved to friends going the opposite direction as she dashed to homeroom. Caught up in the crowd, setting her mind on her first classes, worries about gym class were pushed to the back of her mind.

As hoped for, the first two periods of the day did go well for Anne. Then, it was time for gym class and all the worries contemplated earlier in the morning came rushing back to Anne's mind. Trudging into the locker room, Anne deposited her books into her assigned locker and began changing into the hated gym suit. She couldn't even commiserate with Alice, as her locker was in the last row. It seemed to Anne as if all the shapely, athletic girls had their lockers next to Anne's. Most of them had changed quickly and had already gone to the gym, evidently eager to shoot some baskets. Only Nellie Johnson remained in her row. Attractive, athletic, popular Nellie.

As Anne slipped on her sneakers and tied them, she wondered why Nellie had not rushed out with the other girls. With her long, blonde hair, she was attractive. She was shapely and athletic. She was popular, wasn't she? Anne glanced over at Nellie.

"What are you staring at, Skinny?" Nellie shot at Anne.

"N-N-Nothing," Anne stammered as she quickly stared at her own sneakers, sure she was very red in the face.

"Well, you'd better get out to the gym or you're gonna get in trouble. If I'm team leader, I won't pick you. Of course, no one ever picks you, anyhow. Maybe I'll just tell Miss Zeiders that you were wasting time in here, daydreaming, or something."

With that, Nellie bounced out of the locker room toward the gym.

Anne followed meekly. So, already it was going badly, even worse than usual.

Once in the gym, Anne lost track of Nellie because thankfully, Alice rushed over to her as soon as she came out of the locker room.

"Anne, are you all right?" Alice asked her with sincere concern in her voice.

"Oh, Alice, I hate gym. I know Miss Zeiders is going to pick team leaders, popular girls who will pick their friends, or at least athletic ones for their teams, and I'll be left until the last. It's so awful to be left there, as if no one wants you."

"Oh, I know, Anne, I've been left until almost last also, just like you. It is an awful feeling," Alice sadly agreed.

Now, Miss Zeiders blew her whistle, calling the girls to get into their squads.

Alice gave Anne a weak smile as she walked over to her row near the windows. Anne walked a few paces to her row and sat down on the hardwood floor.

As she expected, Anne watched Miss Zeiders pick the two most athletic, popular girls to be team leaders. Pam Baines and Mary Gardner ran to the front of the gym, next to Miss Zeiders and began calling out names of girls to be on their teams. Anne hardly listened, knowing she would be one of the last to be called. Maybe if she looked as if she didn't care, it wouldn't hurt as much. She tried to nonchalantly glance at the lines and they were as she expected, all the most athletic girls were chosen first. Now, they were left with the non-athletic ones like Anne and Alice. Anne was surprised to see Nellie was one of the girls left. Anne had never really noticed before, only painfully aware that she, herself, was one of the last chosen. Maybe Nellie was as unhappy as she was.

Finally, it was over. Anne was called by Mary, in a rather reluctant voice. Anne took her place at the end of the line next to Mary. Anne glanced at the line and to her horror Nellie was right in front of her! She had figured Alice would not be on her team since she would be chosen last along with Anne, but she had expected Nellie to have been called earlier. Wasn't she popular? Well, she'd have to stay out of her way.

Mary called off the positions and names as their team went to the other end of the gym. Anne was relieved to see that she would be on the side and probably not expected to do much. Suddenly, she realized that, unfortunately, Nellie was on the side also, the same side! It would be harder to stay out of her way now, but she would have to try. It wouldn't do to get involved with Nellie today.

Now, Miss Zeiders was blowing her whistle again, and Anne watched with some interest as Pam and Mary trotted to the middle of the court. Miss Zeiders stood between the two girls and tossed the ball into the air. Both girls jumped up, but Mary jumped higher and forcefully batted the ball toward Joan who pivoted quickly and tossed it toward Karen. In spite of being guarded ferociously by Pat, Karen managed to dribble the ball around her and took a long shot, miraculously getting the ball into the basket! Her team broke into loud roars of "Yay! Way to go," clapping Karen on the back and jumping up and down.

Anne cheered too, smiling broadly at Karen's success, and didn't notice Nellie behind her until she heard a rough growl of "What are you cheering for? You didn't do anything except just stand there." At the same time, Anne felt a hard push on her back and she fell onto the floor with a thud.

Feeling embarrassed, more than hurt, Anne got to her feet as quickly as she could. She figured that probably no one saw Nellie push her and thought she was just awkward and fell over on her own. Things were even worse than she had imagined! Anne decided to not only stay out of Nellie's way, but also to look out for her. She would have to not just be on the defensive, but also be on the offensive!

On her guard for Nellie's bullying throughout the rest of the game, Anne was relieved when Miss Zeiders blew her whistle to signal the end of gym class.

In the locker room, Anne quickly changed into her school clothes while the leaders and their admirers went to the showers with Nellie following behind. In her mind, that was one good thing about not running around. She didn't get all sweaty and wouldn't have to shower today and leave herself open to more embarrassment. She hurried to get her things and to leave before they got back. She'd see Alice later.

On her way to her science class, Anne looked forward to lunchtime. She could talk with Jenny, Alice, and Janette who all ate together now.

As Anne entered the science classroom, Mrs. Kane gave her a warm smile as she always did, which lifted her spirits somewhat. Science had never before been her favorite subject, but Mrs. Kane made it interesting. She gave them projects to do and choices.

As usual, science class sped by and soon Anne was on her way to lunch. She quickly pushed her books into her locker and grabbed her lunch, before dashing off to the cafeteria.

Once inside the door, Anne spotted Alice and Janette in the milk line and joined them. Jenny was purchasing a lunch and would meet them at their usual table at the back of the large room.

"Hi, Anne," Alice called out as Anne came up to the line. "How are you after basketball?"

"Oh, you don't know the half of it," Anne replied. "The basketball was not bad, but what happened before it and during it, that I guess you didn't see, was terrible. I'll tell you all about it when we get to the table."

Once all of the girls were seated at the table, Anne related the story of Nellie's hurtful comments and the pushing in the gym.

Alice was aghast. "Oh, Anne, I am so sorry. I never saw that in the gym. I was at the back of my team and never even saw you fall. I guess there was so much cheering for Karen that no one saw it."

"Well, at least that's a relief," Anne sighed. "I was more concerned about the girls thinking I was a klutz, just falling over on my own than I was at actually being pushed."

Jenny was outraged for Anne. "I can just see that happening. That girl is sneaky."

Janette, kind and quiet as always, expressed surprise. "I can't imagine such a thing happening."

"So, what are you going to do?" Alice asked.

"I think you should tell Miss Zeiders; that girl has got to be stopped!" Jenny advised Anne.

"I don't know," Anne admitted. "But thanks for caring. It really does help just to know that you all care."

"Of course, we care," Janette gently encouraged Anne, as she put a hand on her arm.

When lunch was over, the girls went their separate ways, but Anne felt uplifted by her friends' comments and caring.

That evening, after her homework was completed, Anne began to worry again. The schoolwork all day and homework all evening had kept her mind distracted from the gym incident, but now it was all coming back. What was she going to do about it?

"God, please help me," Anne pleaded aloud. Almost immediately, her eyes fell on her Bible at the back of her desk. She flipped it open and looked in the concordance at the back, under the topic of "anxiety." Scanning the list of entries, she thought, "Have no anxiety..." looked good. She turned to the back of her Bible and found Philippians 4:6, reading, "Do not be anxious about anything, but in everything, by prayer and petition, with thanksgiving, present your requests to God."

The words seemed to quiet her mind and she continued reading, going on to verse seven. The words "And the peace of God which transcends all understanding, will guard your hearts and minds in Christ Jesus" seemed to be just what she needed.

Anne read it all once again, starting with verse four, and it seemed to fill her with a sense of peace. She decided she would try to memorize it in the days ahead and practice the ideas expressed there.

Anne knew this was not going to change Nellie, but for now, the words were helping her to at least give over her worry to God.

With a heartfelt "thank you" to God, Anne could now reflect more calmly on the day's events. She questioned what popularity really was. She decided that only a few people were really popular, like Pat Strickler. There were more like Nellie who wanted too much to be popular and became angry in their attempts.

Anne pulled her diary and pen from the drawer and began writing.

Dear Diary,

Today, gym class was very bad for me. Nellie was very hurtful. But my friends helped me feel better at lunchtime and Mrs. Kane helped me feel better, too. Most of all, God's Word has helped me tonight. I hope I always remember to turn to God.

Love,
Anne

TIME WITH JENNY

"Hi, Jen!" Anne welcomed Jenny as she opened her front door. "Come in. I'm all ready. Just let me tell my mother you're here to get me."

Anne left Jenny waiting in the hall and hurried to the kitchen where her mother was cleaning up after lunch. "Jenny and Mrs. Smith are here, Mom. I'm going now."

"Fine, dear. Thanks for letting me know. I'll be there to pick you up as soon as your father gets home from work."

"All right, Mom. Bye, " Anne called behind her as she rushed back down the hall to Jenny.

"All set, Jen," Anne told her long-time friend as they headed out the door and to the car. "I am looking forward to this day off from school."

"Me too, Anne," Jenny agreed as they slid into the backseat.

"Hello, Anne. Glad you could come with us today," Mrs. Smith called from the front seat as she started the engine.

"Hi, Mrs. Smith. I'm glad I could come too. Thanks for inviting me," Anne replied.

"Boy, this is really a treat, after yesterday," Jenny told Anne as the car pulled away from the curb. "I know you got a polio shot too yesterday. Guess you're okay today?" Jenny inquired of Anne.

"Yes, my arm is just a little sore, that's all. You look okay too."

"Yes, I'm okay today, but last evening, I had a headache. I'm glad it didn't last."

"My parents say a little pain is worth it to prevent polio," Anne responded. "It can be a very dangerous disease. My cousin Carson, who is my brother's age, about twelve, did get polio already and he was in the hospital. At first he was paralyzed. It was bad. Now, he walks with a little bit of a limp. But we all are thankful that he is all right."

"Yes," Jenny agreed. "I've heard of kids even dying from it. So it's better to get the shots."

"Here we are, girls, "Mrs. Smith called back to the girls as she pulled into the driveway. "I'll be doing some cleaning. You go ahead to Jenny's room for a while, but you should get outside too. It's such a nice day. Maybe you'd like to take a walk later. If you want to walk up to the bakery later, I'll give you money for doughnuts."

"Thanks, Mom, sounds good," Jenny replied as she and Anne climbed the stairs to her room.

"Where are your sister and brother?" Anne questioned Jenny as they entered her room where she almost expected the usually exuberant siblings to jump out at her.

"Oh, they're over at the playground with some friends," Jenny answered. "They won't bother us today. We can talk and play records, and dance in peace."

"Oh, I don't mind them. I think they're kind of cute," Anne quickly assured her. "We've been friends now for more than two years and I've gotten used to them."

"Well, that's easy for you to say. You don't have to contend with them every day, like I do," Jenny replied as she riffled through her records. "They're nicer to you. They get into my things and bother me. Here's Ricky Nelson's newest song, "Garden Party." Jenny held up the record and then put it on the turntable of her record player.

The two girls lay across Jenny's bed, dreamily listening to the song. "I really like his voice. It's very mellow," Jenny commented as the song ended.

"Yes," Anne agreed. "And I like the words too. He gives a message if you take time to figure it out. It seems here he's saying to not let things bother you."

"I guess you're right. I never thought about it. I just like the music. I'm going to put on Chubby Checker's 'Twist' next," Jenny told her as she held up another record. "We can practice our dancing for the next dance, whenever that might be."

"That's fine," Anne answered. "Actually, I am going to a dance tomorrow night. You know I go to the Methodist Church. We have a youth group called MYF, for Methodist Youth Fellowship. The Mt. Fern Church MYF is holding a dance tomorrow evening and my mother said I could go. I wish you could go."

"Oh, that's all right," Jenny replied. "I don't know if our Catholic Youth Group will have a dance or not. I hope we do," she added as they danced.

After all the "twists," and "ups" and "downs" of the dance, the two girls fell on the bed, laughing and tired out.

"Let's get that money from my mother and go to the bakery," Jenny whispered to Anne as she heard her brother and sister come into the house.

As the girls passed Billy and Lindy on the stairs, the siblings yelled, "Where are you going?"

Jenny quickly hurled back, "Just out, we'll be back later."

She found her mother in the kitchen washing down cabinets and asked her if they could have the money to get the doughnuts now.

"Sure, Jenny. Now, I want you to get a dozen so everyone can have one tonight. Get that dozen all glazed so there aren't any arguments. Then, you and Anne can each get one of anything you want, to eat on your walk back here." As

FRESHMAN IN '59

she spoke, she reached into the closet for her purse and extracted two dollars, which she handed to Jenny.

"Thanks, Mom," Jenny called back as she headed for the back door with Anne following close behind.

The two girls sauntered along the sidewalk toward the bakery, shuffling their feet in the crunchy brown leaves covering the walk. Soon, they were at the bakery studying the variety of doughnuts inside the glass cases. Jenny asked the baker for the dozen glazed doughnuts and then chose a chocolate one for herself, and instructed Anne to choose one for herself.

Anne also chose a chocolate one, and thanked Jenny.

Jenny paid the cashier, received her change, and gave Anne her chocolate doughnut. She put the box under her left arm and held her own chocolate doughnut in her right hand, taking a quick bite before she headed out the door, which Anne graciously held open for her.

The girls walked slowly back to Jenny's house, nibbling their chocolate doughnuts as they went.

When they arrived at Jenny's house, Billy and Lindy were jumping in a big pile of leaves in the front yard.

Not wanting her brother and sister to see the doughnuts, Jenny hurried past them to the front door, pulling Anne with her. "That looks like fun," she called back to them as she and Anne hurried into the house.

"Wish we weren't too old to do that," she said to Anne as they went into the kitchen. Not seeing her mother, Jenny

59

put the doughnuts and the change in the back of a cabinet so Billy and Lindy wouldn't see them if they wandered into the kitchen. "It seems as if we're always either too old or too young for anything these days," she complained to Anne as they walked by the front door on their way upstairs and heard the laughter outside.

"Yes! I know what you mean," Anne agreed as Jenny put another record on the record player. "It seems as if we're too old to have fun like Billy and Lindy and too young to have fun like babysitting or dating."

As the two girls complained about the state of affairs for girls their age and listened to records, time flew by and before they knew it, Anne's mother was there to take her home. Anne expressed her thanks to Jenny and Mrs. Smith before she followed her mother to the car.

"So, how was your afternoon?" Mrs. Duncan asked Anne as soon as they were on their way.

"It was okay. We played records, danced, took a walk, and ate doughnuts," Anne answered, knowing her mother would want some specifics.

"Well, that sounds better than okay," Mrs. Duncan commented. "Did anything happen that you didn't like?" she added.

"Well, Billy and Lindy seemed to have more fun than we did. They went to the playground and they jumped in leaves," Anne explained.

"Well, why couldn't you two do those things, too?" Mrs. Duncan inquired.

"Mom! We're too old for those things!" Anne shot back.

"It seems to me that if you think they would be fun, then maybe you're not too old for them. On the other hand, the playground was built for elementary school children so maybe it is better to find other things to do. And it sounds as if you did. Did you practice some dance steps you might use tomorrow night at the MYF dance?"

"Well, kind of. The twist is getting popular and it's a little hard to do, but I like it. We did have fun doing that!" Anne answered.

"Well, see there. Maybe you had more fun than you realized," her mother commented. "And I have something else you might think is fun for tomorrow," she added. "How would you like to go to Morristown to shop for a new dress?"

"Really? That would be great, Mom!" Anne exclaimed. "I'll call Sally and Sandy later to see what they're wearing. I wish I could have asked Jenny and her mother what's in style. They go to New York shopping, but since she wouldn't be going to the dance, I didn't think I should say much about it."

"That probably was best, but they are very understanding people, and it's good to have friends of different faiths. It can help all of you to be more accepting of differences and make the world a better place. As far as styles go, Morristown should be a good place to shop."

"Yes, that will be fine, Mom, and thanks. That will be great to look forward to," Anne assured her mother.

That night, Anne decided she had a few things to write in her diary.

Dear Diary,

I had fun at Jenny's house today. Sometimes it's hard being a teenager. We're too old to do some things and too young to do some others. But, we are able to do some things now that we weren't allowed to do when we were younger. I've got to remember that and appreciate it. One thing is that we're going shopping tomorrow and I can pick out my own dress. I couldn't do that when I was younger. And we didn't have youth groups or dances when we were younger. I'm sure there are a lot of good things about being a teenager if I think about it.

Love,
Anne

Dover High School

First Presbyterian Church in Dover

St. John's Episcopal Church in Dover

First United Methodist Church in Dover

J.J. Newberry of Dover, NJ

Library of Dover, NJ

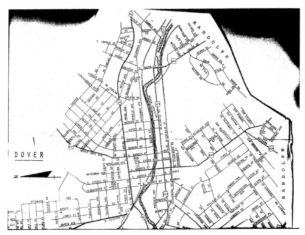

Map pt 1 of Dover, NJ

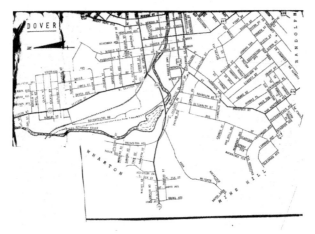

Map pt 2 of Dover, NJ

Diary

Year Book

Rotary Phone

NEW FRIENDS

Saturday dawned bright and sunny, although, as the weatherman stated, it was "seasonably cold." Anne's mother always turned on the TV to hear the morning news and weather forecast, especially before going out driving, this time of year. The first weekend in December, the weather could be so changeable in New Jersey. Today the temperature was hovering around freezing, but no snow on the horizon.

"Looks like we'll have a fine day for shopping," Mrs. Duncan remarked to Anne as she placed a glass of orange juice on the table for her.

"That's great," Anne replied as she poured some cereal into a bowl and added some milk. "Your father and Andrew already ate and left for the barber shop," Mrs. Duncan explained. "They wanted to get there early so they won't be long. As soon as they get back we can take the car to Morristown."

"Sounds good," Anne answered around a mouthful of cereal. She hurried through her breakfast, washed her dishes, and put them in the drainboard to dry.

"I'll go and get ready, Mom," Anne called to her mother who had gone to straighten the living room. She was ready to go a short while later when her mother called to her that her father and brother had returned and she was going out to the car.

"I thought we'd go to Epstein's first," Mrs. Duncan told Anne as they headed up the highway. "Do you know what you want?"

"Not exactly, but I do have some ideas. Most of the girls wear skirts and sweaters to school. But a few of the more sophisticated ones do wear dresses at least occasionally. I've seen several sophomores who are maybe some of the best-dressed wearing some really pretty dresses."

"Well, we'll check out Epstein's first since they're usually more expensive. Then we'll go to Bamberger's and be able to compare prices. We might not need to go anywhere else because they usually have good selections."

"That's true, Mom. They are my favorite stores here. I really like Debuteen in Dover, but since it's so small there are not always a lot of choices."

Soon, Mrs. Duncan pulled the car into a parking place in front of Epstein's.

As they walked past the huge glass storefront, Mrs. Duncan pointed out an outfit on display. "Oh, that's cute," she told Ann, admiring a royal blue belted tunic with a blue and gray plaid skirt.

"It is," Anne agreed. "In fact, I saw a sophomore wearing an outfit like that. I think her name is Cathy and she is definitely one of the best-dressed, but I really think a dress would be nice for this dance and church later."

Walking through the ladies' dress department, they took the elevator up to the second floor, to the junior department. Anne quickly found the dress racks and the size seven section. She scanned the dresses, knowing what colors looked best on her. Her mother favored blue, and with her blue eyes and blonde hair, that was a good color for her. But it wasn't for Anne with her brown hair and eyes.

Anne's eyes fell on a gold and brown plaid dress and she pulled it out from the rack. Those colors together might work for her. Next, she spotted a plain, yellow wool one which had nice lines, but it did have short sleeves. She folded it over her arm with the plaid. A little further down on the rack, she noticed a dark green dress with elbow length sleeves. She didn't know about that color on her, but she really liked the sleeves. She added it to her pile and headed for the dressing room.

"I'm going to try these, Mom," Anne called to her mother who was talking to a saleslady about the dance. "I'll let you see anything that seems good on me," she continued as she entered the dressing room.

A few minutes later she reappeared wearing the gold and brown plaid. "What do you think?" she asked her mother as she turned around for her to see the back.

"It is pretty, Anne, but what about the others? I think I like the green best," she explained.

"I'll try that next," Anne assured her and disappeared into the dressing room again.

About five minutes later, Anne slowly walked toward her mother wearing the green dress. "It really doesn't look good on me at all," Ann told her mother. "I just came out with it to let you see for yourself."

"Well, I do like that color, Anne. It's very Christmassy."

"It may be Christmassy, but it is not a good color for me. I look so pale in it."

"Well, try the yellow one then. Let's see that."

Anne dutifully wore the yellow one out next, but was not happy with that one either. Let's go to Bamberger's," she pleaded.

"All right, Anne. It's right down the block, so that's not a problem, but don't you want to try anything else here first?" Mrs. Duncan questioned.

"No, " Anne answered in a disheartened voice. "I just want to go to Bamberger's."

"All right, Anne, we'll go, but I wish you didn't get so disappointed," Mrs. Duncan replied as she turned to leave.

Anne returned to the dressing room, got back into her own clothes, and quickly deposited the three dresses on the rack in front of the dressing room.

A few minutes later, as they walked into Bamberger's Junior Department, Anne spotted a dress that she admired, on a mannequin. It was a very simple and quiet style with the elbow length sleeves she liked. She really liked the tan and ivory tweed-type material. It even had its own shiny black belt. She was sure she had seen a very sophisticated sophomore named Claire wearing a dress like this one.

Pointing to the mannequin, Anne called to her mother, "I like this one." She scanned the racks for one holding dresses like the one displayed. Finding it nearby, Anne pushed aside a few dresses in size five and found one in size seven. She scooped it up and trotted off toward the dressing room.

"I don't know," Mrs. Duncan mildly stated her opinion, "It looks rather plain to me. I 'd like to see you with something flashier."

"That's just not me," Anne stated as she entered the dressing room.

A few minutes later, Anne appeared to model the dress for her mother. She turned in a circle to show her all sides.

"It fits perfectly, Mom," Anne declared triumphantly. "It comes just below my knees and the sleeves come just below my elbows. The waist is just right, too."

"That is true, Anne," Mrs. Duncan agreed. "It still looks plain to me, but you're the one who has to wear it. But wouldn't you like to look more?"

"No, this is the one I'd really like, I'm sure, if it's not too much."

"It's fine, Anne. I noticed that it is on sale, so if you really like it, we'll get it."

"Oh, thank you, Mom. You're wonderful!" Anne exclaimed.

That evening when Anne modeled the dress for her father, he admired it, too. Maybe having his dark eyes and hair caused him to like the same colors she did, Anne surmised.

At any rate, a short time later, as her mother drove her to the dance, Anne felt confident in the dress. She thought her black flats went well with it because of the black belt. She planned to meet Sandy and Sally there and felt good for all of them because she knew they would have new dresses, too.

Sure enough, when she walked in the door of the fellowship hall there were Sandy and Sally, waiting for her and wearing new dresses. In fact, the dresses looked quite familiar!

"That green looks perfect on you," she quickly told Sally, "With your black hair, it was made for you."

"And the gold and brown plaid looks great with your blonde hair," She enthusiastically complimented Sandy.

"Your dress is really pretty too," Sandy returned, "I really like that tan and ivory mix on you."

"Yes, " Sally agreed. "And it fits you perfectly!"

Caught up in the excitement of new dresses and a holiday dance, all three girls were talking excitedly when one of the youth leaders, Bill Harris, walked to the front of the room and loudly welcomed everyone. They immediately quieted down and gave him their attention.

Bill reminded everyone that the format for the evening would be dancing for about an hour, then a break for a devotional time and refreshments, and another hour of dancing. Then, Bill introduced the youth leader from the Mt. Fern Church. It was a girl with short, shiny hair the color of golden wheat. Anne recognized her from school. It was Maria, from her English class! She had admired Maria, but had not gotten the chance to know her. And here she was a member of MYF! Maria explained the layout of the church building, where the restrooms were located, and the sanctuary to go to later for the devotional time.

As Maria left the front of the room, Bill started the record player, but Anne noticed a girl coming up to Maria. It was Donna! She was in English class with Anne, too. So, she was also a member of MYF.

Anne told Sandy and Sally that she knew the two girls and invited them to go over with her to say hello to them. Sandy and Sally said they were eager to meet them, so the three girls wove their way around groups of boys to get to the other side of the room.

"Maria, Donna, hi!" Anne called out as the three came close.

"Anne!" Maria and Donna chorused together, in surprise.

"It's good to see you," Maria quickly added.

"I didn't know you were a Methodist," Donna continued.

"Yes, my two friends and I are members of the Dover church," Anne explained. Let me introduce you. Maria and Donna, please meet Sandy and Sally," Anne added.

"It's great to have you all here," Maria replied.

"Very happy to meet you," Donna joined in.

"I'm really impressed that you are a leader in your group, Maria," Anne congratulated her new friend.

"Well, it's only because we have such a small group in a small country church," Maria modestly confessed. "And I'm only the vice president. The president is a junior, but couldn't be here tonight. The juniors and seniors work weekends."

"We do have a small group, that's for sure," Donna hurried to admit. "But Maria is too modest. She is a natural-born leader. This dance with your group was her idea."

"Well, it was a good idea," Sandy put in. "But does anyone have any ideas of how to get the boys to dance? They're all hanging around Bill and the record player."

At that, everyone laughed and all started talking at once, suggesting silly ways to get the boys to dance.

"Well, I guess we're just going to have to dance with each other, the way it usually seems to work at freshman dances," Maria decided.

"Well, maybe we're scaring them off, being in a big group," Sandy suggested. "I saw that the punch bowl was out and Wilson went over to it. I think I'll just go over to get some punch and see what happens."

"I'm not so brave," Donna responded as Sandy walked toward the punch bowl.

"Neither am I, " Sally agreed. "I'm for dancing together."

"Yes, let's," Maria replied as she started in dancing across from Anne, and Anne followed her.

Donna and Sally joined in next to them.

As they all enjoyed the music, they noticed Sandy and Wilson come on the dance floor together.

"Guess she was right," Maria whispered to Anne, who just smiled.

They were having a lot of fun when Bill announced it was time to "adjourn to the sanctuary" for the devotional time.

Anne told Maria she knew Bill would do a good job. He was a senior, planning on being a minister, and attending a Methodist college next year.

Seated in the lovely, old wooden pews a few minutes later, Anne studied the simple, stained glass windows as everyone filed in. Bowing her head in prayer with the others, Anne admired Bill's ability to pray publicly. She didn't think she would ever be able to do that.

Anne was equally impressed with Bill's scripture selection and explanation of it. He introduced the scripture reading as Matthew 5:43-48. As he began reading, the words "pray for those who persecute you" seemed to have a personal message for her. Immediately, Nellie Johnson came to mind. Anne had tried to put her and the gym incident out of her mind. She had prayed for peace and was somewhat successful. She had been successful in avoiding Nellie too. But she had to work hard at it and was always nervous if she was near. Now, she wondered if rather than just praying for her own peace, she should be praying for Nellie. She was still contemplating this idea, when Bill announced that they would conclude their service with the singing of the lovely, contemporary hymn "Day By Day."

As everyone joined in singing the simple phrases, the words seemed to go straight to her heart. If she really wanted to love and follow God, shouldn't she be trying to love all people, even difficult people?

Anne continued to ponder these thoughts even as she filed out with everyone else and enjoyed the refreshments. The rest of the evening went by in a haze. She didn't even mind dancing with the girls again.

Anne said her good-byes to her old friends and her new friends too, mechanically. And going home with her mother she answered her questions in the same way. She felt she had a lot to think about.

Before going to bed, she wrote in her diary.

Dear Diary,

Today was a mix of feelings for me. It started out very happy with finding a great dress for the MYF dance. At the dance, my old friends Sally and Sandy met my new friends Donna and Maria and we all had fun. But things got serious for me when Bill led us in a devotional time and I started thinking that I should start praying for Nellie instead of just for myself. I have a lot to think about.

Love,
Anne

SURPRISE PARTY

The following Monday, Anne came home from school to hear her mother talking on the telephone and saying she'd take soda, chips, and pretzels to the church. She finished her conversation quickly and hung up the phone.

"Why are you taking soda, chips, and pretzels to the church?" Anne asked her mother, as she hung her coat on the coat rack and entered the living room.

"Oh, just to help out Mrs. Jones. She's having a surprise birthday party for John on Saturday," Mrs. Duncan answered. "Your invitation came in the mail today, " she added as she handed Anne a small white envelope.

"Boy, that will really surprise him, being four days before his birthday!" Anne exclaimed, as she tore open the envelope and withdrew a colorful invitation.

"Hey!" Anne quickly added as she scanned the invitation. "This says it's at our church, not the Episcopal church. "

"Yes, Mrs. Jones asked if they could hold it there to further surprise John," her mother explained." She knows our church since their church is right across the street."

"Wow! He really will be surprised!" Anne was getting excited for her friend. "When will we shop for a present for him?" she questioned.

"Oh, we'll go sometime, maybe Friday night," her mother answered vaguely. "I need to get supper ready now." And she hurried into the kitchen.

Anne climbed the stairs with her schoolbooks, thinking about the party and wondering what she might get John for a gift. She hoped it might be something a little special since her mother was helping with the party. When she'd found out a few years ago that John's birthday was just three days before hers, she thought that was pretty neat. She didn't have a party every year, so this would be exciting to go to one for John. She tried to put it out of her mind as she opened her history book and began to read the assignment for Tuesday.

The following afternoon, when she arrived home, she was quite agitated as she entered the living room, tossing her books on the sofa and dashing to the kitchen in search of her mother. As she spotted her mother at the refrigerator, she began her complaint.

"Mom, you won't believe what I saw today in the hall at school. I was going to lunch and I saw Joe Baynor talking to John Jones and he was showing John something that looked like the invitation! Maybe he told him about the party and it won't be a surprise!"

"Oh, I wouldn't be too concerned, Anne," Mrs. Duncan replied, "It probably was another invitation or something else."

Anne thought her mother reacted to the news way too calmly. It seemed obvious to her that it must have been the invitation to John's surprise party and that Joe had ruined the surprise.

"You'd better get started on your homework, Anne," Mrs. Duncan instructed. "You don't want to be up late working on it," she added.

Anne left the kitchen feeling that adults just didn't understand what was really important. She slowly picked up her books and climbed the stairs feeling sad that John might know about his party and it wouldn't be a surprise as planned.

Friday finally arrived, coming very slowly in Anne's estimation since she had been eagerly awaiting the chance to shop for a present for John. Her mother had said they would get the gift tonight! She'd already told Anne that Saturday she could wear the white organdy dress she'd gotten a year ago for confirmation. She'd felt so good about that dress for such an important occasion. So, her mother must think John's party was special, too, to let her wear that dress. Maybe that meant they'd buy a special gift, like maybe a record album or even a watch.

After helping her mother with the supper dishes, Anne was expecting her mother to announce that it was now time for the shopping trip, but instead she seemed in no hurry as she walked into the living room to watch the news with Anne's father.

"Mom, aren't we going to shop for John's present now?" she asked her mother, as she followed her into the living room.

"Oh, there's no hurry, Anne. In fact, do you really think you need to get a present?" Mrs. Duncan questioned.

Anne was incredulous as she sputtered, "M-m-mom! What do you mean? Of course, we have to get a present! I'm not going if I don't have a present to give him."

Now it was Mrs. Duncan's turn to look concerned. "You have to go, Anne. If you insist on getting a present, we'll go look in Newberry's as soon as the news is over."

"I'll go upstairs and work on my homework," Anne replied rather sullenly. "I'll be ready to go whenever you are."

As Anne climbed the stairs to her room, she pondered this new turn of events. How in the world would her mother expect her to go to a party without a present? For the second time that week, Anne decided that parents just didn't understand what was important to teenagers.

Later that night, Anne decided parents really were impossible as she wrapped a box containing cufflinks. Cufflinks! When she had thought she might be able to buy something really special like a record album or a watch! Her mother had said that John really wouldn't expect a gift! That was ridiculous!

Then, she had said they really couldn't afford a big gift so she had to settle for something small like the cufflinks. Well, that Anne could understand. Her friends had already started telling her that they would be giving her a combination Christmas/birthday gift. She understood how there were so many expenses at Christmas, but it did seem unfair that she would be giving her friends gifts on their birthdays and gifts at Christmas, too. And she would get a combination gift. Well, she would have to just concentrate on the idea that it was special to have a birthday near the birth of Jesus and not care about gifts. When she thought that way, then gifts really weren't important. But it was hard to stick to that thought sometimes.

Anne went to bed that night with mixed feelings about the party the next night. She had been eager to celebrate John's birthday with him and their school friends, but she wasn't satisfied with the gift she would give him and she was afraid it wouldn't even be a surprise for him. She knew he had joined his church and made the decision to follow Jesus, so maybe gifts and parties weren't so important to him. She just hoped he would have a good time at his own party.

The next day, Anne thought that the day seemed to drag on, in spite of all the usual house cleaning chores. She was almost thankful for them to keep her occupied, but it was too bad that the work only occupied her hands and not her mind. She had plenty of time to mull over all the concerns she had for John and his party. She finally decided to give it to the Lord, asking him to make everything turn out well for John. Then, she did feel a little better.

Finally, the chores were accomplished, supper was over, everything was cleaned up, and Anne was ready to go to the party, present in hand. She couldn't understand why her mother was going so slowly. She'd been in her room getting ready for a while.

"Mom," Anne called. "Aren't you ready? We're going to be late."

"I'll be there in a minute, Anne. We'll be fine," her mother replied as Anne heard her close her door.

When they arrived at the church, Anne noticed several cars parked on the street in front of the church. "See, everyone is here already," she complained to her mother, "I'll probably be the last one to arrive."

"You'll be fine," Mrs. Duncan assured her one more time, as she got out of the car with Anne.

"Why are you going in?" Anne questioned.

"Remember, I'm helping Mrs. Jones," Mrs. Duncan answered.

"I know it's downstairs in the fellowship hall," Anne reminded her mother as she hurried down the hall, opened the hall door, and began descending the steps with her mother close behind her. She was surprised it was so quiet. There must be some people there already. She knew she was a little late. Anne reached the bottom step, and opened the door to the fellowship hall. As she swung open the door, shouts of "Surprise!" greeted her.

Confused, Anne reprimanded the friends, "No, it's John's party!"

Everyone just laughed at her and several yelled, "Surprise!" again.

Jenny was right in front of her, smiling, and assured her, "No, Anne, it's really your party."

Joe Baynor was right behind Jenny, grinning from ear to ear, and shouted, "We really surprised you!"

John Jones stood behind Joe, laughing so hard he couldn't speak.

Unbelieving yet, Anne turned to look at her mother for some explanation.

"Yes, Anne, it really is your surprise party. I guess we really did surprise you."

"Oh, Mom, you sure did, I thought it was a party for John," Anne agreed.

"Well, let's get started with games," Mrs. Duncan directed as they removed their coats and laid them on a pile with others.

Later that night, Anne could not remember all they had done. She remembered they'd had a hilarious scavenger hunt which her team had won. Even though the teams were evenly divided with some church friends on each, her team still seemed to have the advantage of being able to find the items quickly. The memory game was won by Jane Gordon who really exhibited a remarkable recall of all the items on the tray presented to the group. They'd had other games and refreshments and even some dancing. She'd opened presents, nearly all jewelry, suspecting that the boys' mothers must have selected the gifts. And the time had just flown by! She seemed to be in a daze the whole time.

Mrs. Duncan had previously arranged for Jane to spend the night at their home so her parents would not have to make the long trip that evening. Jane and Mrs. Jones were a big help in cleaning up after the party and they were ready to leave the church quickly after the others had been picked up by their parents.

Before they left, Anne thanked Mrs. Jones profusely for all her help and apologized to John for having a party!

John laughed again at Anne's still unbelieving attitude. "Why should you apologize, Anne?" he asked, "I got a gift out of it too. Thanks for the cufflinks. And my mother said that next year, I'll have the party."

So, John seemed to take everything in stride, as usual, Anne observed, and she felt better about the situation.

Anne and Jane talked excitedly in the car as they rode home. Once there, however, their excitement seemed to turn to exhaustion and they seemed to have all they could do to climb the stairs to Anne's room.

While Jane used the bathroom to prepare for sleeping, Anne sought out her parents to thank them for the party and the watch they had given her. Then, she quickly wrote in her diary before Jane returned.

Dear Diary,

I went to John's party tonight, but what a surprise! It wasn't his party after all. It was my surprise party, a week in advance! It was wonderful!

Love,
Anne

THE MUSIC OF CHRISTMAS

The following Saturday, Anne woke up thinking, "Today is December 19; it actually is my birthday, but since the party was last Saturday, nothing special will be done for my birthday today. More than I could ever expect was done last Saturday. What a wonderful surprise party it had been!"

Still, there was something special happening today. Anne would be going to town to sing Christmas songs with her church choir, to be broadcast throughout town. She was really looking forward to it.

Anne hurried through her chores and lunch. Then she dressed warmly and headed to town. As she plodded along on snow-covered sidewalks, she felt a cold breeze ruffle her hair even with her hood up and she pulled the hood closer to her head with one gloved hand. She pushed the other hand deeper into her pocket. Nothing could keep the cold out today.

As she carefully made her way down the long hill, she reminisced about the previous Saturday's events. The party had been the biggest surprise of her life, she decided. She'd had no inkling of what was being planned even though, now, in retrospect, she could see clues had been there all along. There had been the conversation she'd overheard between her mother and Mrs. Jones, then the conversation between John and Joe, the party being held at her own church, and her mother not wanting her to buy a present for John. Now, it all added up, but not then.

Now, having crossed the railroad tracks, Anne felt she could hurry along on the level ground. She wanted to be on time because her choir would start promptly at 1:00 p.m. There would be another choir at 1:30 p.m., so it was a tight schedule.

She turned left at the end of the block. This time she would be going to the Presbyterian church. This church had a tall bell tower where the sound system was housed and it would be exciting to have her choir broadcast throughout the town. She had always loved hearing the singing as she shopped in the local stores. Now, as a high school freshman, she was able to be a part of this wonderful contribution to the town's Christmas celebration.

This was a great way to spend her actual birthday, Anne decided. She'd received lovely gifts from her friends and family last week and now she was able to do something for someone else. She figured that if hearing the music made her heart light, she was sure it must bring smiles to other people's faces.

Climbing the steep stairs to the bell tower, Anne heard low voices chattering above her. Reaching the top floor, she saw Mr. Rivera hushing the group of lively teen-agers as he distributed the music. For this large, unidentifiable audience they would sing mostly secular songs, catchy and familiar to most people.

Anne accepted her folder from Mr. Rivera as she took her place with the other sopranos. She focused on him as she heard a young man operating the sound system announce their choir. Then she blended her voice with the others as he directed them in singing "Jingle Bells," followed by "Winter Wonder Land," and "Frosty the Snowman." With a nod to their faith, they sang "It came upon a midnight clear…" and the words "peace on the earth, good will to men" filled her heart with joy. Then, they ended with the singing of "We Wish You a Merry Christmas."

As soon as their microphones were turned off, they quietly turned to leave and heard the young man naming their church choir and thanking them for their participation as they descended the stairs. As they carefully stayed to the right, another choir was climbing up on the left.

Once outside, the boys slid in the snow-covered edges of the sidewalks since the church custodian had cleared a path down the middle. Anne and the other girls laughed at them, knowing they were just letting off steam as they all had felt compelled to be quiet and serious for the previous half hour.

Mr. Rivera shouted a reminder to all of them to be at their church early the next morning to rehearse for their cantata. Then he watched as Sandy's and Cheryl's mothers pulled up to the curb to pick up their daughters. He watched the others walk down the sidewalk and called a loud "good-bye" to them, before heading back inside the church. Sally and Dorothy were walking home as were the boys and Anne. So, they all shouted their "good-byes" and headed in separate directions toward their homes.

Anne walked slowly, enjoying the feeling of having been a small part of contributing to this lovely community activity. She listened more closely than usual to the music being broadcast throughout the town now. She decided she really liked her small town.

Sunday morning, Anne dressed carefully, wearing the tan and ivory tweed dress. Normally, the choir robes would cover their clothes, but for this special Christmas program the members would not wear the robes. The boys would look good in their suits and the colorful dresses of the girls would make a festive appearance for their cantata.

The choirs had been learning and practicing the music for Handel's *Messiah* all fall. The words, directly from Scripture, were so moving and the music soared majestically. Anne felt so privileged to be a part of this, so thankful that the choir had the direction of such a talented minister of music in Mr. Rivera.

A short while later, as Anne walked with the other choir members into the beautifully decorated sanctuary, she almost trembled with excitement. Sunlight streamed through the large stained glass windows and made the wood paneling and pews glow warmly. The earthy scent of the tall, freshly cut evergreen standing in the corner with its white chrismons reached her nose with a pleasant sensation as she climbed the stairs to the choir loft. The pews were filled with families and yet there seemed to be a hushed silence as they took their places.

All eyes were glued to Mr. Rivera and when he motioned for them to stand, they did it as one body. Mr. Rivera smiled at them in satisfaction and raised his arm to direct them to begin. Their voices blended it seemed as never before. Singing "Lord of Lords" and "King of Kings," Anne felt as if she were really worshipping the Lord Jesus Christ. Her arms felt covered in goose bumps and she sang, along with everyone else, as if she were putting her whole heart, mind, body, and soul into the worship experience.

That feeling seemed to continue as Anne listened intently to the sermon a little while later. Reverend Rodgers was preaching on John 3:16, Anne noted with some surprise. Not the usual scripture for a Christmas sermon she thought, but as she listened, she decided it was very appropriate and very meaningful. After all, she reminded herself, God did send his Son into the world at Christmas. That's what Christmas was all about.

After the service, many adults, especially the parents, and other older adults, complimented the choirs on the music. Anne's Sunday school teacher, Mr. Tanger, came rushing up as she grabbed her coat from the rack near the doorway.

"Anne, that was just beautiful. The choirs sang 'The Messiah' so movingly."

"Thank you, Mr. Tanger. I wish you could have sung with us. You have such a wonderful tenor voice, but I know you have a cold."

"Yes, it was a big disappointment. Will we see you at the Christmas Eve service?"

"Oh yes, we'll be coming, as usual, to the late service at 11:00 p.m."

"Good! See you then."

Anne felt warm all over as she climbed into the car with her family. There were so many lovely musical events at Christmas. And there was another even tonight.

That event came around very quickly when Mrs. Duncan drove Anne to the church so that they both could join a group to go caroling. They would drive their own cars to the homes of shut-in members of the congregation who could not get out to the church to enjoy the music of Christmas. They would take the music to them! It was another exciting time and another opportunity to share with others.

At the church, Sally and Sandy joined them in their car and Mrs. Duncan followed Bill Harris who drove his car with the boys. Behind them, Mr. Tanger drove a group and behind him, Reverend Rodgers ended the procession with the last group.

They first stopped at a small, white house out in the country. Piling out of the cars into the yard in front of the house, they lined up informally and Reverend Rodgers took on the responsibility of directing their singing.

Reverend Rodgers had previously called Mr. and Mrs. Rhodes to ascertain their favorite Christmas carols and now announced that the group would begin by singing "Oh Come, All Ye Faithful." As the elderly couple appeared in the doorway, smiling broadly, the group sang out loudly the popular carol "O Little Town of Bethlehem." They followed with "Joy to the World" and "Hark! The Herald Angels Sing," before ending their program with a rousing rendition of "We Wish You a Merry Christmas."

Cold on the outside, but warm on the inside, Anne joined with the others in shouting, "Merry Christmas!"

Mr. and Mrs. Rhodes waved from inside the door and Mr. Rhodes opened the door a few inches to call out in a feeble voice, "Thank you so much."

It was a scene that was repeated at each of the other homes on their list. Although the cold air made their faces frosty, a warm glow seemed to boil up inside of them as they saw elderly people come to their windows and doors, smiling happily.

After all their visits were completed, all of the cars drove back to the church where everyone enjoyed warming their hands with hot chocolate and filling their stomachs with cookies.

Singing so loudly had made their voices hoarse and the cold air had also tired everyone out, so no one stayed long. Parents came to pick up their teens and Mrs. Duncan and Anne headed home, too.

"We've got a lot to do in the next few days, Anne," Mrs. Duncan told her as they made the short trip home.

"Yes, I know, Mom," Anne replied. "I still have to finish Christmas shopping and then wrap the presents. I know you'll want me to help with the food for Christmas dinner and cleaning the house, too."

"I certainly will appreciate it, Anne. We'll get Grandma to come for Christmas dinner, of course. Aunt Rachel and her family will come early on Christmas Eve, as usual."

"It will be busy, but a happy time," Anne commented as her mother parked the car in front of their house. And, Anne was right. The next three days flew by in a happy bustle of cleaning, cooking, and entertaining her favorite aunt and her family. Anne enjoyed it all, especially the exchange of small presents with her young cousins.

Then, back at church on Christmas Eve, Anne and her family settled into a pew halfway down the aisle. The younger families would have attended the earlier service; now, the church was nearly full with the teens and their families, young couples, and singles without children.

Singing the wonderful hymns again, Anne thought she never could get enough of them. Singing "Joy to the World" and "Joyful, Joyful We Adore Thee," Anne felt her heart would burst with joy.

Reverend Rodgers opened the pulpit Bible to the old, familiar story of the birth of Jesus, in Luke 2. There were Mary and Joseph going to Bethlehem, the angel appearing in the fields to the shepherds to announce the birth of the Savior—all of it was just marvelous.

The best part of it for her, and probably for others too, Anne mused, came with the singing of the last hymn. The traditional singing of "Silent Night" in the darkened sanctuary, as the congregation held candles they lit from each other, was just so moving and peaceful. The words "sleep in heavenly peace" seemed to create just that atmosphere. Everyone seemed moved as they sang quietly but with much feeling. When the lights came back on and the candles were extinguished, the silence was broken. But, even as people wished each other a "Merry Christmas," the feeling of peace seemed to still be with them.

That peace seemed to envelop them as they came out to their cars. Midnight seemed very special tonight. It was the birthday of the Lord Jesus Christ!

Anne hurried to write in her diary as soon as she got to her room. She didn't want to lose that feeling. She wanted to record it and remember it. She wanted to have it with her always. She quickly took out her diary and pen and wrote.

Dear Diary,

The Christmas season is filled with music for me. Common, ordinary, lively music like "Jingle Bells" makes us happy, but the old carols and hymns really fill us with deep joy. I really wish Christmas could last all year.

Love,
Anne

A LONG, COLD WINTER

As the February break from school came closer, Anne and her friends all seemed very much in need of a break from the routine. They often spoke at lunchtime of looking forward to the time off from school. Anne thought she and Jenny might do something together.

"It has been a long, cold winter," Jenny complained when she appeared at Anne's locker after school the day before the break. "My parents said we all could go to New York for a few days," she added.

"I'm glad for you and your family," Anne quickly replied, trying to be polite. Her heart sank, however, because she'd really been counting on doing something with Jenny.

"What will you be doing?"

"I really don't know," Anne answered honestly.

"Well, I hope you can find something new and interesting to do," Jenny kindly offered. "I'll see you next week."

"Bye, have a good time," Anne answered as they both turned in opposite directions down the hall.

As Anne pulled up her hood, put on her gloves, and marched out into the bitterly cold afternoon, she contemplated the next week and the break. She thought of Jenny's words. What could she do that would be new and interesting? She came up with nothing. It looked as if the long, cold winter would be reflected in a long, cold week for her next week.

Trying to shake herself out of her mood, Anne decided she really didn't want to feel so "down." So, she prayed, "Lord, I don't think you want me to feel this way. Please help me to find something worthwhile to do."

Feeling somewhat better, Anne climbed long, hilly Morris Street toward home. Her heart seemed lighter as she looked forward to what new and interesting thing the Lord might bring to her.

Anticipating something good would happen soon, Anne was able to call out cheerfully to her mother as she entered the hallway of her home. "Mom, I'm home!"

"I'm over here in the living room, Anne," Mrs. Duncan answered from the far corner.

"What are you doing?" Anne questioned as she hung up her coat, put down her books on the steps, and headed for her mother who was kneeling in front of the book case.

"I'm cleaning out the old magazines. My *Woman's Day* magazines are piling up. "It's so hard to get rid of them. I always think I want to get back to some article, story, or recipe, but they have to go. I'll cut out some things, but the rest has to go. Why don't you go through your *American Girl* magazines and do the same?"

"Okay, Mom. I'll take a stack up to my room. I don't have much homework over the break so it'll give me something to do at least for a little while."

With that, Anne picked up a stack of her *American Girl* magazines and her books and headed up the stairs.

Placing the two textbooks on her desk, Anne settled on the bed with a magazine. It was the December issue and filled with colorful photos of Christmas scenes, decorations, and activities. December had been so busy that she hadn't really looked at this issue very well at all. Now, she could take her time, go slowly, and read it all.

Two hours later, Anne was ready to put the magazine aside. It had been a pleasant respite, but it was time to help with supper she realized as she glanced at the clock. Just as she flipped to the last page, she noticed something she hadn't seen before. It was an announcement of a writing contest.

The announcement encouraged teenagers to enter short stories they had written. The stories could be fiction or non-fiction and had to be less than 1,500 words. The deadline was February 28, so she still had time. This was only February 19. Tomorrow was Saturday and she had all of next week to work on it. Surely, that would be enough time to write a short story.

Wow! That would be something new and interesting, she reflected. But, could she do it? She liked writing. English was usually her favorite class. But, could she write a story worthy of a contest? Well, why not try? It couldn't hurt, even if she didn't win. It could be fun just to try. Now, what would she write about? That was the big question.

Anne pondered that question all through supper preparation, eating with her family, and even cleaning up. She told her family about the contest during supper. As she expected, her mother encouraged her to enter the contest. Her father and brother teased her.

"So, you're going to be a writer!" Mr. Duncan said.

"Well, I don't know about that. Just writing one story for a contest doesn't make me a writer. But, I thought I might try since I don't have anything better to do. Besides, there is some prize money. Not a lot, ten dollars for first prize and five dollars for second prize, but it is something. And, it might be fun."

"Writing for fun? Boy, you must be crazy. Nobody I know thinks writing is fun. In seventh grade we have to write stories every week for Miss Baines, and it's not fun," Andrew put in.

"That isn't very polite, Andy," Mr. Duncan reprimanded.

"That just shows the difference between us," Anne responded. "I really liked those writing assignments Miss

Baines gave us. I thought it was fun cutting pictures from magazines and making up a story about the scene or person pictured. And Miss Baines liked my work. I usually earned an A."

"Well, bully for you. I'd rather be outside sledding than wasting time inside, that's for sure," Andrew threw back at his sister as he got up from the table.

"Your brother has always been an active, outdoorsy type of person," Mrs. Duncan commented as she rose with plates in her hand and moved toward the kitchen. "You have always been more sedentary, liking to read and to write," she explained.

Anne followed her mother with her own and her father's dishes. As they washed and dried the dishes, Mrs. Duncan asked her what she thought would be her topic.

"I really don't know. I have read that it's best to write about what you know or have experienced. That doesn't give me a lot to work with," she laughed.

"You'll think of something," Mrs. Duncan assured her.

Anne thought about the contest all evening, but she still didn't have any ideas until she was getting ready for bed and thought about her diary. Deciding she did not have anything of interest to write in her diary, Anne asked herself what was the last interesting thing she'd experienced. And then, it came to her. Her surprise birthday party! That was certainly interesting to her and maybe it would be so to readers.

Anne fell asleep thinking about her idea of writing about the surprise party and woke up Saturday morning contemplating it further. While she worked on her chores, she considered how she would begin the story. The easiest thing to do she decided was to write it just as it happened and submit it as non-fiction.

As soon as her chores were completed, Anne started in on her story. She decided that she would start it from the time she received the invitation and relate all the things that had happened that she now viewed as clues. Having it at her own church and her mother helping should have seemed strange she thought now, but it didn't then. I must be very gullible, she thought, and wondered if anyone reading the story would catch on to what was coming, or if they would be fooled as she had been.

Right after lunch, Anne began writing, even though her mother urged her to get outside for some fresh air. She really enjoyed the writing and didn't enjoy being outside by herself. No one her age lived nearby. Jenny was in New York, Alice was visiting relatives with her family, and Janette had a lot of work to do. This writing—getting down on paper all that had happened in an enjoyable experience—made her happy. It was like reliving it all over again.

The only thing that bothered her was that the writing made her hand hurt after two hours. Whenever she finished the story, she would have to wait a day to rewrite it so she could submit a copy in her best handwriting, she told herself. Jenny had gotten a typewriter for Christmas, but her other friends didn't have one. Maybe she would try to take a typing class over the summer and ask for a typewriter for next Christmas. But, for now, she would have to write it out. The contest rules had stated that stories could be handwritten or typed. So, this was acceptable, but hard on her writing hand.

Anne went to bed that night tired but happy to be doing something creative.

Sunday went by quickly with church activities and visiting with Aunt Rachel's family. Anne was eager to get back to writing but glad to have a rest.

Then, it was Monday and Anne was back to writing again after lunch, when the telephone rang. Mrs. Duncan called to her from the living room and Anne ran to answer the call, glad for a diversion.

Picking up the telephone and saying hello, Anne discovered Alice on the other end of the line.

"We just got back from visiting and I wanted to see what you were doing," Alice kindly inquired.

"I've been busy trying to write a story for a contest."

"Wow! That's great. I know you'll do a great job," Alice encouraged her.

"I hope I can, but even if I don't win, it's still fun trying," Anne responded.

"Yes, I can understand that. You do like to read a lot and so, writing kind of goes along with that. In fact, I was wondering if you'd like to take a break and meet me at the library."

"That sounds like a good idea. I do need to take a break. My hand is hurting. My mother wanted me to get outside so this will be a good way to do it."

"Great! Can you be there in about an hour?"

"Yes, I'm sure I can. Just let me check with my mother."

After checking with her mother and telling Alice that it would work, Anne put away her writing materials, put on her coat, and walked down the hill to town. She did not mind the cold as she hurried along. Going to the library was a good idea.

As Anne approached the last block to the library, she saw that Alice was already there, waiting outside for her. That made sense, as Alice did live closer to the library than Anne did. She did not want Alice to wait any longer in the cold, however, so she hurried her steps even faster.

"Hi, Alice," she called out as she came nearer. "Have you been waiting long?"

"Oh no, not at all How is your story coming?"

"Well, I did get started, but it seems to be going slowly. I know my topic now, but figuring out what to put in and what to leave out is difficult. How was your visit with the relatives?"

"It was the usual. I do like going to see my aunts, uncles, and cousins, but I don't like the long ride with my little brothers and sisters. It's always good to get back home."

"I know what you mean. It is cold out here. So, even though we can't talk in the library, maybe we'd better get inside. Did you want anything in particular?"

"Not really. I just like to get any fiction, especially books about girls our age."

"Yes, I do too. I especially like books by Betty Cavanna and Anne Emery, but I like just about anything that seems realistic. I've ordered Scholastic books through school by authors I'd never heard of before and they've been very good. How about you?"

"I especially like mysteries, like the ones by Carolyn Keene and I like classics of girls who lived long ago, like those by Louisa May Alcott," Alice explained as the two girls climbed the steps to enter the library.

"I've got an idea. Why don't I try one of your favorite authors and you could try one of mine," Anne suggested in a whisper as they opened the huge, heavy doors.

"Sounds great," Alice whispered back as they headed to the young adult fiction.

For the next hour, Alice and Anne helped each other in finding books. Anne also decided to borrow a book of short stories "to try to get into the hang of it," she explained.

After checking out their books, they burst out laughing when they closed the doors and descended the steps.

"Boy, it's a relief to be able to talk normally again," Anne told Alice. "I think I'm going to like this book by Louisa May Alcott.

"And I think I'll enjoy this one by Betty Cavanna," Alice put in. "Let's check with each other in a few days. I'm sure I'll be busy with my little brothers and sisters, but maybe I can get to some reading in the evenings."

"All right, it will be fun to compare notes," Anne agreed. "Talk to you later," she added as they walked off in opposite directions.

The next few days flew by, Anne was surprised to discover, as she read and wrote. The first time she wrote her story, it turned out to be 1,800 words. So, she made the introduction more succinct and ended the story earlier, at the point where she was surprised instead of at the end of the evening. She was able to get it to 1,250 words.

On Friday, Anne took her time copying her story in her best handwriting. After lunch, she put it into an envelope and dropped it into the corner mailbox. She would not hear the results of the contest until April. That was a long time to wait.

As Anne came back into the house, the phone was ringing and she grabbed the receiver off the hook. "Hello?" she inquired into the phone.

Finding out it was Jenny, back from New York, Anne asked how the trip had been. It sounded as if the Smith family had really enjoyed their week in the big city, shopping and seeing Broadway shows. Anne was happy for her friend.

When it was Anne's turn to share her week's adventure in writing for the contest, she was disappointed to find that Jenny did not share her enthusiasm for writing. She hung up the phone feeling as if she had wasted her time.

Later that evening, Alice called and inquired about her reading and her writing experiences in the past week.

"Did you get your story done and sent in on time?" Alice asked in a concerned voice.

"Yes, I sent it in today. Thanks for asking," Anne responded.

"That's great. I know you put a lot of effort into it. I do hope you win a prize."

"That's very kind of you, Alice. I would like to, of course, but when I was writing it I enjoyed it and thought that was enough."

"That's a good way to think," Alice replied. "How about your reading? How do you like Louisa May Alcott's writing? I really liked the Betty Cavanna book."

"I am so glad that you suggested it. It is different from the contemporary books I usually read, but I really did like it. I like the slower pace of that period of time."

"I am so glad, Anne. I have to go help with supper now. I'll see you at school."

"Bye, Alice. Thanks so much for calling," Anne ended the call reluctantly.

Later that night, Anne reflected on the different reactions of her two friends as she wrote in her diary.

Dear Diary,

I finished writing my short story for the contest today and felt good about it when I mailed it. When I told Jenny about it, she did not seem interested and I felt disappointed. When Alice called and was interested, I felt much better. I think that I need to be satisfied for myself and not depend so much on what other people think. I need to realize that people have different interests and be glad that I have a variety of friends. I hope I am maturing.

Love,
Anne

SPRING AND RESOLUTION

Beautiful, tiny purple crocuses sprouted up everywhere at the end of March, and Anne felt her spirits lift. Spring had finally arrived. Sledding and ice skating had been fun, but she'd had enough of the ice and snow. She looked forward to enjoying the outdoors more, especially the flowers and little animals. Squirrels, rabbits, and chipmunks scampered around the backyard seeming to enjoy the sun as much as she did.

Anne took a deep breath of the warm, fresh air. She was helping her mother with the laundry early on a Saturday morning. As she hung up clothes on the line outside the back door, she admired the little flowers. This was a chore she didn't mind at all on such a lovely morning.

When Anne came back inside, her mother was talking to someone on the telephone.

"Fine, thank you for calling," Mrs. Duncan was saying. "I'll have Anne call you back right away."

As Mrs. Duncan came toward Anne in the kitchen, she explained, "That was Mrs. Watkins on the phone. She wanted to know if you would like to go with them and Betty to a farm tomorrow afternoon. You'd come home with us as usual after church. You'd have time to eat dinner and change your clothes and they'd pick you up about 2:00 p.m. What do you think? I said you'd call them back."

Surprised, Anne asked, "Why are they going to a farm? Where is it?"

"It's in Sussex County, near Newton, only about forty-five minutes from here. It belongs to the owner of the plant where Mr. Watkins works. They've been invited there for the afternoon and will stay for supper. They've invited you to join them. I imagine they thought Betty would like the company."

"I guess I could go. They are such nice people. I don't know them really well, but I see them all the time at church and we have been to their house a few times. I think I'd like seeing the farm. Since Betty is a year older than I am, I don't see her at school much, but when we've been at their house she's been friendly. I'll call them and accept the invitation."

Anne picked up the receiver and dialed the number her mother had written down for her on a notepad by the phone.

As soon as Mrs. Watkins answered, Anne told her, "Mrs. Watkins, this is Anne. I really appreciate your invitation to go with you to the farm. It sounds like fun and I'd love to go. I can be ready at 2:00 p.m. tomorrow. Thank you for asking me."

"We're so glad you can join us, Anne," Mrs. Watkins kindly replied. "Betty will be very glad for the company. We'll be at your house at 2:00 p.m. tomorrow then."

"Thank you, again, Mrs. Watkins."

Anne hung up the phone and told her mother it was all set.

As she contemplated what she would wear the next day, Anne climbed the stairs to get her clothes ready for church and the farm adventure. "I am looking forward to it," she whispered to herself. "I think it really will be fun."

The next afternoon, Anne was ready and waiting when Mr. and Mrs. Watkins arrived to pick her up. As soon as the car pulled up to the curb, Anne yelled a quick "good-bye" to her mother and dashed out to the car, climbing into the backseat.

After the greetings, Anne and Betty settled down into talking about school.

They soon found out that, as a freshman in the business program, Betty hadn't had the same teachers that Anne now had.

"How is gym class for you, Anne?" Betty asked. "You must have Miss Zeiders as your teacher. Is she still as gung ho as she was last year?"

"I guess she is. She seems to really like the athletic girls and that leaves me out," Anne replied. "It's the worst class for me; I'm glad we only have it three times a week."

"Me too; I hate gym class with a passion," Betty commiserated. "But at least sophomores get Miss Berg. She isn't so geared toward the athletes. She doesn't do that picking team leaders thing. She picks two teams herself and no one is left standing there waiting to be called. I was always last and hated it."

"Boy! Do I know!" Anne quickly agreed.

From the front of the car, Mrs. Watkins overheard the conversation. She inquired, in a gentle, concerned voice, "Have you girls thought of praying for this teacher and telling her how you feel about how teams are chosen?"

"I haven't prayed for the teacher or told her how I feel, but I have prayed for a certain girl," Anne answered.

"That's wonderful, Anne," Mrs. Watkins responded. "Have you seen a difference?"

"I can't really say that I have. She still seems mean, but I try hard to stay out of her way."

"That sounds like a difficult situation. Isn't there something more you could do?"

"I don't know," Anne mumbled.

Concern in her voice, Mrs. Watkins pointed out, "The Bible gives us an idea."

She continued, "In Luke 6:27, Jesus tells us to not only love our enemies, but also to do good to them. Why don't you look for a way to be especially kind to this girl?"

As Mr. Watkins pulled into the driveway of a big, red, brick farmhouse, he spoke for the first time. "We'll be praying for you to find an opportunity, Anne."

Anne felt really touched that they cared so much. "Thank you, Mr. Watkins," she choked out, with tears in her eyes.

The next two hours went by quickly as Anne and the Watkins family were given a tour of the farm and enjoyed a bountiful supper. Anne found the goats to be the most interesting animals and was amused at their antics. When she was invited to drink some goat's milk with her supper, she eagerly accepted and felt it was a treat.

Later that evening, when Mr. Watkins parked the car in front of Anne's home, he reminded her of his promise to pray for her to find an opportunity to be kind to Nellie.

"Thank you so much for everything," Anne replied as she jumped out of the car. "I really enjoyed the trip, and your prayers mean a lot to me."

The next morning, Anne was a little less apprehensive about gym class as she changed into her gym suit in the locker room. She prayed that she would find a way to be kind to Nellie.

Following the routine she had adopted after the fall incident, Anne hurried to change clothes and to get into the gym so that she wouldn't be left alone with Nellie. She didn't think she was going to be able to do anything much in the locker room. She would look for her opportunity in gym class. She couldn't imagine what could come up there, but trusted that Mr. and Mrs. Watkins were praying and something good would happen. She believed God would provide an opportunity. She would just have to be looking.

As Anne came into the gym, Miss Zeiders blew her whistle to call the girls to get into their squads. She was in a hurry today, Anne guessed. She and Alice didn't even have time to talk as they usually did. Alice was waiting for her just outside the locker room door, but as the whistle blew, she smiled, waved, and ran to the other side of the gym to get into her squad. Anne walked the few paces to hers.

After taking attendance, Miss Zeiders said she was going to do things a little differently today. For the softball teams today, she would be choosing two girls who then could choose the two team leaders.

Anne was surprised. This was different. Then, she became even more surprised when she heard Miss Zeiders call out her name! Next, she called out Alice's name! She and Alice would be choosing the team leaders!

Miss Zeiders asked Alice who she would like to be a team leader. Alice looked uncomfortable, but looked around the room at the expectant faces. She finally announced the name of Mary Gardner. Everyone seemed to smile in satisfaction as Mary ran to the front of the gym.

Then, Miss Zeiders called on Anne to choose. Anne had been thinking while Alice did her choosing. She knew what would be expected. Everyone would expect her to choose Pam Baines or another athletic girl. But, Anne knew what she had to do. This was certainly her opportunity. She loudly announced the name of Nellie Johnson.

Anne was sure she heard soft whispers of "What?" and "Who?" She saw the faces of Miss Zeiders, Mary, and Alice looking surprised. Then she glanced at Nellie as she slowly made her way to the front of the gym next to Mary. Nellie looked as surprised as everyone else, but in a very happy way. A big smile brightened her usually sad face.

Teams were chosen as usual. Nothing changed in that. Mary and Nellie each wanted her team to win. Alice and Anne were still chosen last. But, this time Anne didn't really mind it.

At lunch time, Alice asked Anne about her choice of Nellie and understood her explanation.

"I think that was very kind of you, Anne," Alice praised her friend. "I do hope it works and Nellie is nicer to you. Did she thank you?"

"No, she didn't thank me and I don't expect it, but I do hope it helps her to be kinder even for her own sake. She can't be a happy person the way she was acting."

That night, Anne continued to feel good about what she had done. She decided it was a great feeling to be able to "do good for your enemies." Maybe it would even turn an enemy into a friend. She decided this was a time to write in her diary.

Dear Diary,

Today I tried what Mr. and Mrs. Watkins had suggested. I tried to "do good for an enemy." Miss Zeiders gave me the chance to choose a team leader and I chose Nellie. I hope it made her happy and that she becomes a kinder person for her own sake. I know I feel good about what I did and I hope she can do kind things so she can feel good about herself.

Love,
Anne

THE BUSY
MONTH OF MAY

"We really need to hurry if we want to get to all three stores," Anne told her brother as they left the J.J. Newberry store for the W.T. Grant store a few blocks away.

"Tomorrow is Mother's Day and I want to find something good for Mom," Andrew retorted. "And I'm not going home until I do."

"Well, I want to find something good, too, but we don't have a lot of time, or a lot of money, either," Anne explained. "Do you really want to get her a bracelet as you said? Newberry's certainly didn't have anything you wanted."

"No, they didn't, and I know just what I want. It has to be really special. Mom is letting me keep my snake in the laundry room."

"Yeah, I know! I am not going anywhere near that laundry room if I can help it."

Arriving at the store, Anne led the way to the jewelry counter. She was sure she wouldn't find anything she wanted here. She was counting on the J.C. Penney store to have something she might give her mother.

As Andrew looked over all the bracelets, Anne thought about how she also really wanted to get her mother something special. She recalled how her mother had taken her and Jenny to Boonton to look for an Easter dress. They'd visited a number of stores and she had gone home with two dresses! When she couldn't decide between the green cotton dress and the beige flowered one, her mother had said she could have them both!

They'd had such a good time that day. But, Jenny had seemed distant lately. Just yesterday, after lunch together, she'd wanted to stay inside and Jenny had decided to go outside. More and more lately, it seemed that they had different ideas and interests.

"Nothing here!" Andrew announced. "Let's go to the next store."

Her reverie broken, Anne readily agreed and she quickly followed her brother who was already on his way out the door. At least Penney's was right next to Grant's.

Again, Anne led her brother to the middle of the store to the jewelry department. This was where she hoped to find something nice for her mother, so she looked at the tops of the display cases and inside them too, very carefully. She wished she had more money to spend, but even with the allowance she'd saved and the babysitting money she'd earned, she still had only five dollars. But, she couldn't complain. She had been given three dollars for the babysitting job. Andrew had only three dollars all together since he didn't have any way to earn money yet.

"Hey! I found it, Anne. Look at this. Mom will love it." Andrew said joyfully, pointing to a shiny, rhinestone bracelet.

It wasn't Anne's taste, but if Andrew liked it, their mother probably would, too.

"All right, Andrew, let me look some more," Anne directed as she turned the corner at the end of the long glass counter, still looking hard for something she could buy.

Just as she was rounding the next corner, almost at the end of the jewelry department's glass display cases, Anne spotted something she really liked. In a small velvet-lined box, was a set of black and white cameo earrings and a pin. It would take all her money, but it was on sale and definitely worth it.

"I found what I want to buy too, Andrew. Let's take our purchases to the cashier," Anne instructed her brother as she picked up the box.

"Oh boy! I can't wait to see her face when she opens the box tomorrow and sees that bracelet," Andrew enthused as they carried their purchases home a short while later.

"Yes, I'm sure she really will like the gifts," Anne agreed.

Once home, Anne volunteered to wrap both gifts and to hide them in her room until the next morning. Andrew was glad to have his sister do the wrapping, but insisted on having the gift he'd purchased hidden in his own room. It was good to see him so excited about giving their mother a gift, Anne thought as she returned the gift to him now wrapped in bright flowered paper.

Sunday morning, after breakfast, Anne invited her mother to go to the living room to open her gifts. Sitting on the end of the big gold and blue plaid sofa, Mrs. Duncan smiled expectantly.

Mr. Duncan followed and sat in his favorite brown-covered rocking chair next to the sofa, reaching behind the chair and pulling out a large, rectangular, white box and laying it on his lap.

Andrew ran over to his mother and, thrusting his gift into her hands, entreated her, "Open mine first."

Mrs. Duncan tore off the wrapping, opened the small white box, and pulled out the rhinestone bracelet. It glittered in the morning sun streaming through the long windows behind the sofa. She held it up for everyone to see and then placed it on her wrist.

"Thank you, Andrew!" Mrs. Duncan exclaimed. "It really is beautiful. I'll wear it to church today."

Anne got up from the other end of the sofa and handed her mother the gift she had for her. "Happy Mother's Day, Mom," she quietly announced as she moved to the side.

After tearing off the wrapping and opening the small, black box, Mrs. Duncan pulled out the cameo pin and earrings.

"Thank you, Anne. They're very lovely. I'll wear them to church today too."

"Oh, Mom, you don't have to wear them today. You could wait for another day. I'll understand."

"No, I want to wear all my lovely jewelry today," Mrs. Duncan assured Anne.

"Here, Anne." Mr. Duncan stretched out his hand holding a box of candy, to his daughter still standing near her mother. "Please give this to your mother."

As Anne handed her mother the box of candy, she remarked, "You did well, Mom."

"I guess I did, Anne," Mrs. Duncan replied. "You all have been very generous. Thank you so much."

Anne reflected on that happy time the following Tuesday as she joined her classmates in the cafeteria to take the essential battery tests. Maybe thinking of something happy will help me to relax and to do my best, she mused as she sat with the test on the table in front of her.

At the command from Mrs. Kane standing at the front of the room, all of the students opened their test booklets and began reading.

Two hours later, the command was given to stop, put down their pencils, and close their booklets.

Anne wiggled the fingers of her right hand. They'd gotten cramped from holding her pencil tightly as she had concentrated and tried to work quickly.

Being told that they could now get their lunch, Anne rose from the table and looked around. Donna, who was only two seats away, waved at her. Anne walked over to her.

"What did you think of the tests, Anne?" Donna asked. "I thought the math was hard, but the reading seemed pretty easy," she added.

"I felt the same way, but then English always has been my favorite subject," Anne agreed.

Just then, Maria came up to Donna and asked, "Are you ready to eat?"

"Why don't you join us, Anne?" Donna invited.

"That would be great," Anne answered enthusiastically. "I have my lunch right here," she explained, pointing to her lunch bag.

"We usually bring our lunches also," Maria joined in. "And we usually sit in the middle of the cafeteria, right down here a ways. Is that all right with you?"

"That's fine," Anne replied. "I'd love to eat with you. I usually eat with other friends, but they're in other classes and will have their tests this afternoon. So, thanks so much for inviting me to join you."

Anne later reflected on how much she had enjoyed that half hour. Since Donna and Maria were in her English class, they were able to converse about that class, all that they had been reading, and doing in there. They even talked of studying together in a few weeks for the final exam. She felt really happy with these new friends.

The next day, Anne ate lunch with Jenny, Janette, and Alice. Janette said they had missed her the previous day. It was good to be back with her old friends. She felt comfortable with them.

At the end of the day, during the last period class, Anne was interested in an announcement, which she heard over the intercom. There would be a GAA assembly program in the gym the following day just before lunch. Students would leave their classrooms when called to go to the gym. It sounded interesting, but Anne didn't know what it really was all about. As she walked to her locker, she saw Alice.

"Hey! Alice, do you know what that GAA assembly is all about?" Anne questioned her friend.

"Oh, yes, I know what it is," Alice answered. "GAA stands for Girls Athletic Association. Girls do routines related to their sports. My sister Belinda is on the drill team and has been rehearsing every afternoon this week for their part in the show."

"Thanks, Alice, for telling me. It sounds like fun, although I'm not athletic."

"Yes," Alice agreed. "You know I'm not athletic either, but it should be fun to watch and we get out of class to go! Well, I have to hurry to get home. See you tomorrow!"

"Bye, Alice, see you then," Anne called after the vanishing Alice.

The next morning, Anne was at the end of the line filing into the gym with her classmates. She'd left her history book on the rack under the desk and had to go back for it. Now, she needed to sit next to another class. But, isn't this a girl she'd seen before? Anne smiled at her, but said nothing. Throughout the program, Anne wondered where she'd seen her before and what her name was. She was petite and pretty, with short, curly, black hair and a lovely olive complexion.

As soon as the program ended, the girl solved the problem. She turned to address Anne.

"Hi! I'm Lorraine Blecker. I think we met at graduation last year. We were wearing the same pink dress."

"Oh, yes! I remember," Anne enthusiastically replied. "This is amazing, that I see you now and haven't seen you all year."

"I guess we're in different classes. Are you going to lunch?" Lorraine asked.

"Yes, I am," Anne answered. "I usually meet some friends by the entrance to the cafeteria. "Where do you eat?"

"We eat by the exit, so that's why I haven't seen you at lunch. Would you like to eat together today and get to know each other?"

"Thanks, that sounds great, Lorraine," Anne agreed.

Following Lorraine, Anne stopped on the way to the cafeteria to retrieve her lunch bag from her locker.

Once in the cafeteria, Lorraine introduced Anne to her friends. Pat had long, straight blonde hair, Sue had short brown hair, and Cathy had very curly, long blonde hair.

Anne joined Cathy at the table since she had brought a lunch. Lorraine, Sue, and Pat went to the cafeteria line to buy their lunches.

When they returned, everyone talked excitedly about the GAA program, classes ending soon, and summer vacation. The girls asked Anne to join them again tomorrow.

Telling them about her friends, Anne was invited to bring the girls to all eat together. Anne agreed that she would ask and maybe all would get together on Friday.

The next day, when Anne extended the invitation to her old friends, Alice was glad for the invitation to join the others. Jenny and Janette weren't so sure. They finally decided they would try it.

On Friday, all eight girls ate together near the exit of the cafeteria. There was much laughter, joking, and sharing of stories of their freshman year. Everyone seemed to be looking forward to summer vacation.

That afternoon, Anne reported to her mother that they'd "had lots of fun."

"Did everyone get along well together?" Mrs. Duncan inquired.

"I think so. I met Janette, Jenny, and Alice at the doors to the cafeteria and took them over to the other end to meet the others. I sat next to Lorraine with Sue next to her, and Cathy and Pat were across from us. Janette sat on my other side with Alice across from her and Jenny was at the end of the table. I couldn't really see her very well, but everyone seemed happy.

"It certainly sounds nice. I'm glad you are making new friends but sometimes it's hard for a lot of different people to all get along together. Just be aware and don't push."

That evening, Anne reflected on so much happening in the past month. A lot of changes had transpired in this past year, her freshman year. Last September, she had been worried. She had come to ninth grade with a few good friends and now she seemed to be making a lot of new friends. She hoped she could keep them all, the old and new.

Soon, her freshman year would be completed. Summer held a lot of promise. Sophomore year would be even better, she was sure. She took out her diary.

Dear Diary,

Last year at this time, I was really worried about the coming year at school, being a freshman, wondering if I'd make new friends. I've been making new friends and one girl I think will be a good friend is Lorraine Blecker. She seems very interesting. I am looking forward to the summer and being a sophomore.

Love,
Anne

CPSIA information can be obtained at www.ICGtesting.com
Printed in the USA
BVOW08s1116220315

392750BV00016B/262/P